LEMURIA (MU)

The Mysteries of Khan Gu

The Great Initiation

Signet IL Y' Viavia: Daniel

I

Table of Contents

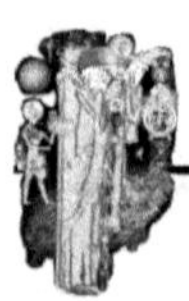

Dedication

I have clean hands and a clean heart. . . Whether I live or die, I would be glad to preserve my honor—Francis Bacon

On Easter Sunday April 16, 2017. *Lemuria, (Mu) and the Mysteries of Khan Gu, The Great Initiation,* was first dedicated to the appropriate theme of Death and Resurrection and to Christ, and to the rebirth of spring and to those Long-Livers, referring to those who are the liberated living, whose long lives have contributed so much to the world. Among those who deserve their Easter to be named in this resurrection honestly are: Francis, Anthony and John.

Anthony Bacon's Easter Sunday April 22, 1601.

Sir Francis Bacon's Easter Sunday, April 12, 1626 and to his sacrifice on Easter Sunday in 1621.

To John Dee's Easter Sunday, April 5, 1608.

To the many also who came from Cambridge University following Easter Sunday in 1630, whose brave souls gathered their last that Sunday, before they set about to sail to America to found the colony in the harsh wilderness of Boston Bay and established their first Puritan, Neoplatonic, Masonic and RC University dedicated to the legacy of virtues, and the founding of all those towns around New England, in the Great English Migration that set down the roots for the foundation for the United States of America, with their ideal vision of the Golden Dawn, of what was to come with the Golden Age in their vision of God's Kingdom.

And, finally to Bhagavan Sri Sathya Sai Baba whose Easter Sunday was April 24, 2011.

This work was completed however, not on April 16th as planned but on April 23, 2017 which was one week late from my target date of April 16th or Easter 2017. It was not completed until the week following Easter. One thing after the other, and another day was

added. It was a week of adding this, rewriting that, rereading, missing, changing and rereading, pulling out the old notes from the 1970's, remembering this, until finally it finished itself, by this hand, and by his publication date.

I say this because, it was not my plan, but it became obvious by midweek, as I was reminded that the following Sunday was the day celebrating Sai Mahasamadhi. By Saturday night April 22nd, as desperately as I tried I gave up, and realized, it could not be done yet.

No matter what I did, and how hard I tried, it would not be finished until HE said it was finished, and that was Mahasamadhi. Every day I tried desperately to get done, and he wouldn't let it finish.

And so, this work is also dedicated to the theme of truth, honesty and virtues. Without such encouragement, love and inspiration, nothing of this would make much difference, as HIS hand was in it.

This work is first and foremost the theme that is dedicated to: Morality.

But our memory also turns to Sir Francis Bacon who deserves a special place in this initiation, [*and since the auditorium where this was first played was named after him*], so we quote the following, and this particularly for those who have forgotten truth in support of national lies in their false quest to dishonor him.

We say, he would make all other past sage histories of the worlds greatness's seem little more than a footnote in history, if the great truths behind him, his brother and friends were ever told, but that would be impossible. No encyclopedia could contain them. He was the Vyasa, who could not (cannot) die.

He was called by them "Apollo Sun" the son of Pallas Athene. He was for some, that long-lived Bombadil and true author of The Great White Brotherhood that still supports the liberated living,

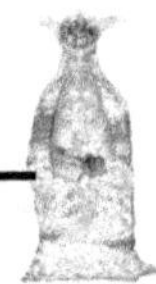

and its founding members, even after 500 years:

"I loved the man and do honor his memory . . . In his adversity, I ever prayed that God would give him strength for greatness he could not want. Neither could I condole in word or syllable for him, as knowing no accident could do harm to virtue, but rather help to make it manifest." —Ben Jonson re: Francis Bacon

"For my name and memory, I leave it to men's charitable speeches, and to foreign nations, and the next ages; and to mine own countrymen after sometime be past." —Francis Bacon's Draft Will.

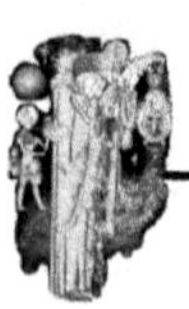

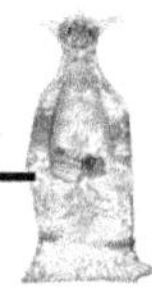

Introduction

"If ever the light of God descended upon any man in this century, it was upon His Lordship, for although he was a great reader of books, his knowledge came not from books, but from some deep, hidden source within himself."—Rawley on Sir Francis Bacon

Here begins what might be meant as legend. The format itself is written as a novella initiation for the Akshaya Patra Series. There is a magical undertone to be certain and one imagined that follows the Tree of Life. That is meant to be. The imagery for this is in the Tarot of that series.

These may be difficult however for even those who are at their philosophical best. Maybe no one will ever read it. Though it does not take much genius, but because of the use of language, the concepts or the vast cultural differences in the method. I have lost faith in humanity otherwise. The majority are quick witted or academic. Not today, but for a Golden Age.

The language is meant to be melodic and at times poetic, though I am not a fan or nursery rhyming. Those have value for remembering. It is meant to be spoken out loud as in the original, in live audience. It is easier to read it aloud as honest reflection since it is written entirely as oration. It is a creative method to make it come to life, by the mind, breath and voice. It forms many prescriptions for autosuggestion.

That method gives it a place that is not "*common*" and therefore it gives it a sacred place. In its suggestive language, as one may imagine, it is a prescription for the mind and its subject of seeing into, or beyond the world of senses. In that sense it is a mental and spiritual medicine.

To one a stone may be a rock to another it is the crowning achievement of excellence. It is not alone imagination. That truth is hidden in it. This is written not for today, but for the entry into the Golden Dawn during the Golden Age of Man as seen by the

Puritan, Cathar, or Gnostic at the same end of what is in the East Kali Yuga.

The creation of the initiation and the ceremonial aspects are simple and they are evocative or invocative, for their purpose of suggestion. No word ever spoken has been without a suggestive element. But this is for your benefit.

The concept of Time is extremely difficult when attempting to convey a message. These concepts are beyond the conceptions of modern physics even as ancient as they are, since they imply profound insights for self-knowledge and dedication. Here's why:

- Time comes from the future and not the past. In Kabbalah, it is the science of future seers or the prophets. Time is conceived as YHVH.

  The first statement of the Genesis, "*Bereshith Bara Aelohim,*" inferring the creation of the six days means literally that "*in the beginning the gods,*" formed the Heavens and the Earth, at that instant of creation, which was followed by the emanations of the six active and one passive periods of Time.

  Whether that is to be considered a *"Big Bang"* theorem or not, it is the energy of Binah the third sephirah or spirit, which is the same energy of Intelligence that ends in forming the tree of spirits from the Godhead of Super-consciousness.

  What we discover empirically is the vibration and radiation of the twin properties of the Electromagnetic Spectrum, or the table of vibrations that form the Cosmic Keyboard and the Cosmic Consciousness.

  This is what exists in the formation factory called the philosophical cosmic egg (*Hiranyagarbha*), or the Galaxy of galaxies, as also in the solar system, planets or energies all the way down to the nucleus of the atom. It is in effect the same as the *Miracle of the One Thing*

themed *As Above, So Below*. Or, as Solomon would say, it is the *"No New Thing Under the Sun,"* because it is always the *"One Thing"* miracle.

The Earth is the spermatic germ within the cosmic egg. Therefore, in truth it is an Earth-Centered universe, as Truth is told, in the Miracle of the One Thing. If for nothing else than that the center of every living thing is the center of the universe. *"I do not live in the center of the sun, but the center of the earth. That center rests in the center of my chest that is within me. In my space, I am the center of the universe."* That should be the common mantra for the true mystic, because that is where, for us, God exists in its nearest and dearest state.

The name associated with the Hebrew Prophetic practice is the same as that of the Yogi, "ASR," (*Aleph, Samekh, Resh*) or Asar as one that is yoked, and it is also the name for one who is captured *"In the Beginning."*

That would be both the ideal mentioned as Man and gods, with that binding of the branches that form the paths uniting the limbs on the Tree of Life, which is bound together within a single Cosmic Hierarchy as a divine community.

ASR is the same root as Ashram which in Hebrew means *"to Bind"* or as they say *"to Yoke"* or yoga. ASR or Asar, is also the Hieroglyphic name for Osiris. And also, the name for the immortal gods "Sura" who are imprisoned as mortal gods and divided within the vitalities in Man, or "not-gods" called the "A-Sura." These are the divisions of Osiris who is cut up and divided.

May we for a moment simply be unbound by those who

teach by saying simply *"Repeat after me."* This is not academics.

The lineage of the Twelve Prophets are called the Trei-ASAR *(the Old Testament prophets that were twelve and they were collected representatives, representing the ancient traditions and oracles)* and the name is seen in the name of God as, *"Eyeh-Asher-Eyeh,"* or *"*I Am THAT I Am,*"* where *"Asher"* is also said by some, to have been the actual name used for the ancient Hebrew name for God. This would imply also a root in Assyria, or it may be also Asar or Osiris. It would imply that the twelve prophets were also devotees of Osiris as was Moses when he describes the "Burning Bush" or Tree of Life as Kundalini.

If you substitute A for Y *(Aleph and Yod)* or the one for ten, you have Asariel instead of Israel meaning the God Asar. In Hebrew Kabbalah there is an equivalence.

Samekh *(S)* as used in ASR gives it the same word meaning as the Pythagorean Greek word coined as Cosmic *(Ka-Samekh, implying the soul of the universe, using "S" as opposed to Shin "Sh." (The Ka and Ba are the soul and spirit principles from hieroglyphic Egypt.)*

The letter Shin represents the three fires or spheres of the triple crown i.e., Kether, Chokmah, Binah meaning the Crown, Wisdom and Understanding, where Intelligence and Wisdom can also be representative of the universal aspects of Spirit-intelligence and Soul-persona.)

AShR would mean to be advanced or blessed, also to be the saintly or blessed, or to be the guide or teacher, as in *"the heart as a guide"* for the wise as seen in Proverbs 23:19, referring to AShR that is to be directed by this, or inferring that it is the Director as well.

In Freemasonry, ASR is symbolized by a rope used to bind one by the cable tow. What does God bind? The Heart or divine center, from which one can never escape, even in death. Also, the vow that he hears either voiced, sworn or contemplated in prayer.

In Jeremiah 46:4, ASR is used to mean *"to harness,"* as we would say *"to harness the horses,"* and this means also, when referring to the senses as horses, meaning *"to harness the senses."* Similarly we might also say, *"to bind our enemies,"* which are also the senses.

When the Hexagram is added (Vav) as in the days of creation, it becomes a place of binding or a prison house or place where one is held (ASVR).

- The entire cosmos is nothing compared to the Soul or Atma itself. That is called "space" however reaching out far beyond that boundary of stars. It is not an infinite depth. It is one that is Eternal. Time exists only within the boundaries of the Cosmic Egg or the Cosmos (*Hebrew:Samekh*). That to it is nothing more than a twinkle.

- We think of space as dark light, but it truth it is unreflected light that is everywhere omnipresent.

- The Aeon vibrating, cycling, or orbiting, is a time creature. It is a state of supreme intelligence in a vast state of super-consciousness.

- One who knows Kabala should understand the Tree of Life (YHVH-Aelohim) is the time creature. In spirit, that becomes man as Archetype and Intelligence, and is flushed out as the form of the Universal Man. That is the creature of attributes, personalities and qualities.

In time these unfold as aspects of genii or genius, angelic forms or time periods (angles) of

superconsciousness, as timed aspects of the cycle. The archetype is a universal or over-arching creator. As that, it is not Self-Created but rather it is a created universal aspect of creation out of the ONE, and it is the seeded aspect or spermatic element forming, not alone driving concepts of ideation, but the ideation of ideal creation in all of its changing forms.

There can be no evolutionary change that it is not responsible for. Those original concepts of Darwin were in fact according to these principles insane. That can easily be proven.

- The descent from the Crown (1) called Kether to Malkuth (10) called The Kingdom, exist as globes in creation; or the subtle to mortal layering of the Cosmic Egg.

They are whirling spheres or planes of consciousness as well as periods of time (Aeons), descending or falling in condensation or gravitation, as mirrored in the concept of the "Fall," or finite "materialization" of elements, cosmic bodies, cellular elements, or creatures incarnating into mortality, falling from their higher state, into the finite world of form.

- The center that is everywhere and nowhere is the gravitational tonic around which all motion returns once it is created. That is also the fall, since it attempts to fall back into the nonentity or God.

There, God is placed in the center of every form whether atom, plant, creature, animal, man, planet, sun or star or star system, galaxy or the entire cosmic (*Hiranyagarbha*) that is conceivable as a singularity, or one single state of awareness, or as the One Thing, sometimes called, "*The Beast.*" On the Tree of Life, God is seated in Chesed Glory, and the Beast in

Geburah or *Severity*, being the one who conceives.

This detailed book is based upon an earlier version of a short play written in 1978 which itself was adapted as a rewrite of a very, very short play presentation written by Ralph M. Lewis, Imperator of The Rosicrucian Order, AMORC.

I was given the task of producing and directing it. The professional actors refused to play it in that condition and so I was forced to rewrite it and present it back to Mr. Lewis in the new rendition.

He didn't like the idea of rewriting his "masterpiece" but he lost the argument and we produced it.

The play was based somewhat upon the book Lemuria, Lost Continent of the Pacific, by Wishar S. Cervé (Harvey Spencer Lewis with the letters "Le Pen" removed).

The play itself was used by the members for demonstrating Rosicrucian Principles and practices on stage, as a magical theme and demonstration, and it was acted out on many levels of human reality, that are here unseen and unreported.

The methods used when staging the magical demonstrations were based on those principles taught by Frater Watermeyer who was of the caliber of the GWB.

As well, Lamar Kilgore, a dear friend, came in on as Saturday and demonstrated the capabilities of the Rosicrucian principles to all those who acted in it.

Lamar came in and effectively ascended and vanished in the cloud in front of those who witnessed it. He also demonstrated the ability to breathe a cloud of light from the breath.

These were practices taught within the Rosicrucian monographs though very difficult for those who were beginners.

A few of those sitting in the council in our play however were very advanced in their practices. This art form is called the Rosicrucian Cloud. The end or object of this is the state called the Divine Assumption, or that quality losing the little "I" identity, and merging into that state of divine self-identification (Eyeh Asher Eyeh) as the state of pure awareness, as being One with it, when losing body consciousness, or that cold jail of the senses.

Many of the descriptions as well were personal. They were actual experiences of mine. They were actual dreams and visions seen in meditations during, or prior to, the period of the original writing of the play.

The experience of the Great Mother, Ana-Anta Hoa-Ana Hacoma Mer-E-Yam, was an experience that I had when at AMORC. I spent several weeks rearranging the pattern of the Enochian letters of John Dee's elemental tablets into a single tablet.

The pattern was changed according to the division and direction of the elements moving from the center of the spirit, and fanning out like a galaxy moving from the center and based on the original tablets of the elements, called the Enochian Tablets.

After completing this Table, I lay back in meditation, and the Great Divine Mother appeared in a vision to me, in that borderline state, between waking and sleeping in a state of pure awareness, and in that state, as mentioned in this book, she gave a profound discourse.

It was beyond my understanding at the time, but the Obelisk at first rose out of the waters, and the surface was blank stone, and she waved her hand over it and from where she sat upon her throne the obelisk was covered with strange writings, and these were written and translated in several archaic languages, one above the other.

This was somewhat like the emerald tablet or that tablet form known as the Rosetta Stone.

Besides the chanting and forming the field of letters upon the plane which cut through the sea of chants, she began to explain the meaning written on the obelisk.

I made foolish demands that I regret, for speaking and not understanding. She, frustrated but decent, as easily translated these to English and explained them to me with regard to the letters and number meanings.

She was very real and quite beautiful and she was, as you can only imagine, far more than any words here could possibly describe.

The flood scene in the play originated with the play but it was enhanced since it is based upon what I saw when I was originally writing the play when attempting to see into the past during meditations.

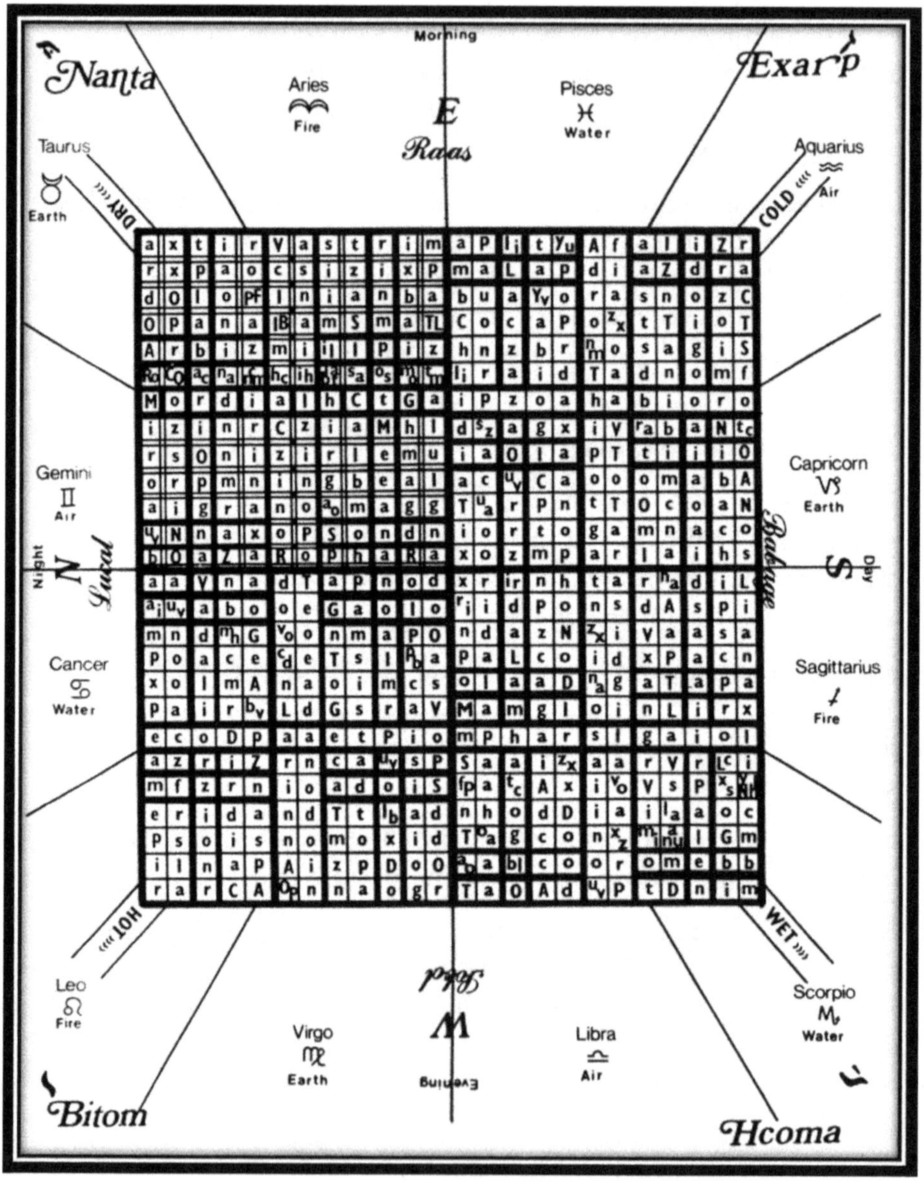

Nanta
Exarp
Bitom
Hcoma
Morning
Aries
Fire
E
Raas
Pisces
Water
Taurus
Earth
DRY
Aquarius
Air
COLD
Gemini
Air
Night
N
Luxal
Capricorn
Earth
Cancer
Water
HOT
S
Day
Sagittarius
Fire
Leo
Fire
Virgo
Earth
Evening
Libra
Air
Scorpio
Water
WET

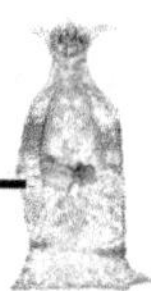

I couldn't say truthfully if it was past memory or imagination, but the situation I found myself in was very real. Although to clarify, in the scene of the devastating fall of the continent, and the flood that I saw then, the waves were so high they came in higher than all the buildings by tsunami and it was several hundred feet high, and also there was a huge very bright colored pyramid that was centered in front of me, and that was covered with beautifully painted symbols that were filled with meaning, as were all the buildings.

As the waters came in, it was clear that death was obviously immanent. It literally took my breath away and it was quite frightening. I came out of it immediately.

To help understand this, there are many different elements that are written into this novella initiation developed from the play that are too much to explain. The magical elements are quite real as seen in the invocations and evocations.

It is written in the syntax of having been written in translation from another time and another language. This is quite natural in the intuitive writing, and it is evocative and takes you to another time and place.

To give an example would be to look at Attra on the stage. It is possible to see these formations described during invocation and evocation.

The open uncovered temple is the ideal, since it is open to the stars or played before the gods. When one swore oaths in ancient initiations, they did these under the open sky, being sworn before the gods (*stars at night*). To swear an oath under a closed rooftop meant that it was subject to be a lie, because it was not given before the gods.

The language method as well, as mentioned, is in the form of invocation and is targeted as you would a hypnotic prescription,

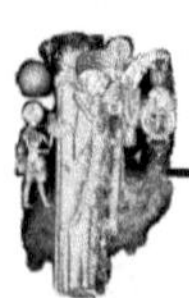

and that form is meant to be suggestive to the subconscious and cosmic mind in order to trigger the mysteries and their universal insights, and follow the symbolic elements. The inner mind reads through symbolic meanings of complex imagery. These symbols collect and grow, live and have meaning, divine number, power, purpose and emanation or communication. Their purpose is to take you to God and Liberation.

The roots in the mystery language use Words whose elements are rooted in Mayan as well as those of the Mauri of the Pacific Islands, Hebrew, Sanskrit, Greek and many other sacred languages.

If you know or research these, you will find the path to their originals easily. AL-Ham for instance is very specific to Kundalini and the Hebrew Tree of Life as A-L-H but it is enough to move energies between the sacred eye (Aleph), to the throne seated at the coccygeal Muladhara (Lamed), and Vishuddha (Heh), which is the Akasha or Sound Brahman, as a purification practice.

The method uses the Kabalistic Tree as the ideal image behind the fall of creation into form, since it is meant to be an initiation as a symbol descending in Time as the archetype of time (YHVH). We see in these sentences the use of the sephiroth in the language of the spiral forms that are given in specific scenes, particularly those attributed to Time as in Crown, Wisdom, Intelligence, Glory, Beauty, Victory, Splendor, Severity and Kingdom etc.

It is difficult to explain the depth of this to those who live in the mindset created by mundane academics. Time is the third Sephirah called Binah, and it is equivalent to the Demiurge or Tetragrammaton.

We are this, and this is within us. It is the same as the second Brahma, as creator god or as the form of the Triad of the first three sephiroth.

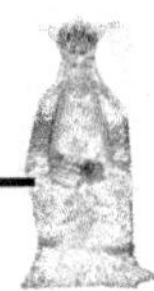

This is the first manifestation of God in existence, or the states of motion, cycle or vibration. It forms the supreme Intelligence and Wisdom that rises far beyond the senses as the subtle, recondite or occult nature.

But to know this in its original cause, one must become it, or attempt to form it, and then step into it. This requires privacy and time and is not that easy to perform. It is the divine form of the universal magical cause/effect, in our lives, that is omnipotent, omniscient and omnipresent.

There is no difference between us. We are one with it.

Time is the live periodic motion of vibration, cycles, orbits, gravity etc. These move, and are held and communicate through the power of their centers. That center is the seat of God.

The universal Zero entity is the cause of gravitation, or the spirit in these centers of attractive power, in the dual forces continuously driving through in the push-pull of galactic forms.

[This was partially explained by Walter Russell and Theosophy through physicists who were Theosophists around the late 19th and early 20th Century. Theosophy is rooted in Thomas Vaughan's writings. Thomas Vaughan, if known in truth rather than history, was one of the identities played on the world stage by Thomas Vagan, who was the long-lived Imperator and founder of Freemasonry and Rosicrucianism in England i.e., Francis Bacon. These were established for his group of Prince Favorites, as the son of Queen Elizabeth.]

We are living in these centers within the Cosmos. One, is a singularity, which is the equanimity that is the same everywhere, in every center. In the center that is everywhere and nowhere.

They (*the gods*) are found in centers representing the qualities, which are the divine characteristics, that are hidden, yet exposed, by the zero state of the universal centers, as powers that motivate the galaxies, or the nucleus of atoms, and as well all globes that

make appearances; like the suns, planets and moons, (*or not, i.e., as in globes that are invisible to senses*).

You have duality as seen in magnets. There is either the attraction or rejection (push-pull) in the field. The fields are One and none. Two opposing poles come together and these magnets attract and matter will come together, and space will collapse between them.

There may be thousands of magnets, but only one field and one center. In opposition, the space between like polarities is a field and that matter, in empty space, cannot be invaded or collapsed into that center. It is impossible to consider since they will fly apart.

That center is always sacred in the field in either case, and the field is always One, a singularity in spite of the many objects that make it up.

It is the fact of the divine center, that forms the odd miracle of the neutron star. What is gravitational collapses, but there is a desire for all that energy to pass through an impossible center, where all parts want to collapse to zero in an instant, and therefore the density and the magnetic field become insanely powerful in their proximity to God.

God is the attraction in the center that draws energy to it and holds it in place or causes it to move apart.

The entire cosmos is seen as the mind of God, or the finite form of superconscious energies that are as alive as the synapse functions that form in a vast entity or beast.

That system or unity, transports superconscious desire and exchanges that desire by the will to self-create through divine Wisdom and Intelligence in the exchange of power.

We may only glimpse and imagine it. It would be very difficult to know it. We're not talking about the mathematics, but the

assumption of its nature as experience.

Each Sephirah, [*united Sephiroth, SPYRT, or spirit*] is a global sphere that is anywhere and everywhere the model for that center that is omnipresent. Every animate and inanimate object has a spirit center. Those that are active and alive simply show there is divine life active within the center, whether a plant, creature, animal, man, planet, moon or star.

The divine life is either active or passive in the zero-state center. We simply say *"animate or inanimate"* life, since they all have properties of Light.

Animate life is inspired by Love. Those inanimate may also be inspired by those who Love. They store those properties as would metal in contact with a magnet.

This is why they can be charged to take on states of consciousness as are amulets or magical implements, or leave behind a record formed of the energy of the touch (*as felt by one sensitive who can feel the history of the handler, as a record by the touch.*)

That zero center is God and we discover that it is that zero state of energy that outer energy cannot pass through, or the zero-pass-not or naught, of the nonentity i.e., Ain-Sof/Brahman, or that webbed knot, in the transition of its energy, that attempts to move through its centers, that are united throughout the Cosmic Universe, contributing to the clockwise and anticlockwise movement of powers, in all galactic properties whether in an atom, star or galaxy.

So, it has to go, come and return, as a property of its momentum, which contributes to the lightning speed, which is called its winged "Mercury."

The powers called *"planets"* are all life properties (*pranas*) of motion, like those found in the days of the week or hours of the day or days of the year or the seven-periodic season of the year.

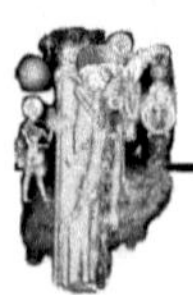

They are time periods divided by seven or roughly 52 day periods in the year, or the periodic divisions of the day that contribute to the energies of planetary rotation.

What is animate in motion, cannot cross into the zero-state or it will be annihilated, as it might attempt to in, for instance, a black hole, or at that opposite, the miracle of an exploding star, where its energy attempts to die and collapse into its center, to try and pass through the crown of Kether through that gravitation, but instead it forms a super nova as a form of death and reincarnation.

The zero-state is laughably the concept stolen in the capture, or production of the subject of "anti-matter."

There, in zero, God as well is identified as the nonentity or AinSof/Brahman.

[This subject of the Supernova's interference in the Zodiac, is the astrological meaning or object of complaint hidden in the opening the Sonnets, said to be Shake-Spear, that complained of the supernova that occurred in 1604, which effected nativities which ended the Tudor legacy, associated with Francis Bacon, saying "Thou that are now the world's fresh ornament and only herald of the gaudy spring, i.e. the Sun in the nativity, buriest thy bud in thy content and maketh waste in niggarding."]

We may laugh, but God appears as well in the center of the creation of a classical nova when forming a star.

The kabbalistic spheres or absolute centers are the Spheres of Chokmah-Wisdom and Kether-Crown, which are both timeless and eternal states, as also THAT, or "*Tatwam Asi, Tat Savitur, I Am That I Am*" beyond, that is called the Ain Soph Aur or Brahma as Brahman in the primeval nonexistence. This Ain Sof Aur is equivalent to the first Brahma as Brahman in translations.

It is one thing to talk about them, but it is quite another to become them.

The word "Glory" refers to that power of God in Chesed on the Throne of Creation. It is God's incarnation into the cosmos as it is the first "day" of the seven days of creation.

The two opposites, Chesed and Geburah are the spheres of the King and Beast.

After Binah Glory is the center of what is conceived of as that principle of Jupiter, or the first benevolent untouchable divine incarnation, seated on the throne, below the trinity. It is the downward seeing Lord as the Avatar or Prajapati. It is the Lord of the Fall or Hanged Man. It is the One that is capable of incarnation.

Its divine name is "AL" in Kabala and is shown as the inverted form of the Fool in Tarot, or the Hanged Man, the one fallen or the one inverted and hanging, and held by the Tau, by a cable tow, which is why he is seen in the sign of Sulphur, or the inverted number four, representing the soul as the King or Emperor.

Although seen as prajapati the creator-father, demiurge, or as the creative lord it is seen in the hanging letter "M," and in Hebrew it is identified hidden by three letters "LMD," to include the Law in lawful Justitia and the King (the letter "L" or LaMeD as the Lawful Word, or Libra-Letter-Light-Love-Life of the liberated Universal King or Emperor).

In the Kundalini, the identification with Glory is with the Son of God Ganesha, literally seated on the throne or Muladhara or coccyx. But this says too much but refers to the seat of superconscious energy.

The atmosphere versus Atma-sphere in the text is used to emphasize the difference between the atmosphere and space.

These two words are used to clearly identify the region of the life winds that surround the world, versus the region we commonly refer to as space or "outer space."

This Atma-Sphere, is the breathless state. Our common word used for this is to signify simply *"space,"* but that is mind numbing nonsense, since it is the Akashic entity beyond our sphere of life energy.

In the Sanskrit, this Atma-sphere is equivalent to both Akasha, and the Sound Brahman, as well as the soul's surround or Atma. In man this is associated with the throat or Vishuddha.

We think of these in our foolish terms based upon our mirror of the senses. These are written here as the causes existing as they are ideally meant, being the life of the ONE Thing, as that under the earth, on the earth and beyond the earth, moving through the sun, planets and stars and beyond, into that endless depth beyond the cosmic creation i.e., as in Gayatri featured as Bhur, Bhuvah, Suvaha Tat Savitur etc...

The child's face appearing above the altar in the ritual scene is microprosophus, or the Ze`ir Anpin, the lesser countenance or small face, as the mirror reflection or revealed aspect of God who is ever youthful.

La Mayach, referred to by the council in the play, is the decision to send the group to the Mayan state or lower world, similar to Malkuth, and it is referred to in history also as Malkata, in the hieroglyph, and that refers to the Palace of the King, or Kingdom of God.

Malkata was the name of the Royal Palace and it is used in that sense as a name, when it was inhabited by the lineage associated with the 18th Dynasty, or Thutmosid Dynasty, originating from the early Egyptian 14th century BC. It was a palace occupied there in Egypt until the Roman-Byzantine Period.

Malkata was the seat of the Western founding of the Mystery Schools of Thutmose III.

The divine state of Malkuth is the pure state that surrounds the Earth. It is that kingdom of *La Mayach* or the Maya. We have seen those images of the image of the Mayan Temples in Egypt as well as pointed out by Abd'el Hakim Awyan.

We might think of this, as well, as the meaning for the mirror of illusions stemming from those subtle first vibrations that are unseen but self-creating energies, or the unreal illusions of motion (*or simply Mula-prakriti signifying the root, base, foundation or source as seen and also the descriptive name of Mal-Kuth, which means the root source of Kuth or life.*)

Malkuth is not the "solid" composting earth as mentioned here in the text, but rather that universal immortal state beyond that. That is referred to by Franz Bardon, as the Zone Girdling the Earth. The RC writings of Thomas Vaughan speaks of this in alchemical details.

You will find in the language of the text some Hermetic references, as well as those of the Druids and Paracelsus, some astrologic analogies, and also those spirits referred to alchemically in The Secret Teachings of the Rosicrucian.

I used all resources available at the time when this was first written, on the subject of Lemuria and those Mayan sources such as the legends of Queen Mu. The true object of course is not to write history, or make a mockery of it, as much as it is to formulate an initiation into sacred mysteries that have a practical method and catechism, and to create a ritual that is one that communicates on many levels. We don't care about the history here. It is a platform for the Mysteries.

This story is not unlike the Tree of Life in Kabala and the rites promulgated by the Kabbalists who were Melchizedeks or righteous kings.

You have divine mysteries integrated into family trees as the royal identity of Monarchies that have their roots in the ancient mysteries, or those connections that once existed honestly, between the sages, saints and ruling royal families.

From these Pacific Island nations one can imagine the migrations east and west. Migrations east would have been to places like South America and Easter Island perhaps, and the like. Migrations west would have been through the Islands of Malaysia through south Asia, perhaps Australia, India and into Mesopotamia and Egypt. These would have a relationship with the Rama Empire and the Hebrew migrations, as well as the legends of the Solar and Lunar dynasties.

Like these, the Hebrews migrated because they had lost their kingdom. Although described as the sons and daughters of Eber, their legacy goes far back into Kashmir and southern India, through Tamil Nadu and beyond Sri Lanka.

Here these scenes are not meant to be specific or true to history but true to initiation. The cultures of South America are as ancient as any in Africa if true histories recorded were told, but they do not fit into academic narratives that are censored in the Universities.

The language invokes principles associated with divinities on the Tree of Life, as universal principles of divine intelligence, associated with the fall or condensation into material form.

The magical statements in the form of sacred letters have kabalistic value and the methods move energies deliberately through the sympathetic nervous system and have meanings hidden by the letters. They communicate with the Kundalini.

The Self, conceived its primal cause, as manifest in the principle of divinity and conceived through mythology in its virginity, as the completed form in musings. A word of knowledge escapes the memory, but a picture of knowledge is easily recalled, it lives and grows and carries with it the intuition, and the essence of subconscious and superconscious elements that form reality.

These in turn effect more easily the areas of mind and brain to recall mundane sensibilities, enabling the greater increase in occult

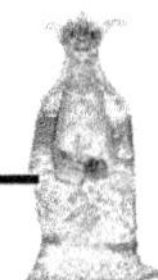

or subtle powers of perception. The theater now is simply filled by fools covered by their books and conceived in cowardice.

Consciousness in truth, is the "matter" of life, and that is conceived or caused by Superconsciousness that comes from the radiations of the suns.

This of course, is simply the mundane explanation and it is meaningless to many, but it helps to play on the sentiments for deeper understanding.

The story is presented here to tell much more than this, and to evoke more than is presented. Don't be fooled into thinking about this in the objective sense. That isn't the purpose of it. In fact, it would be the dumbed-down sense since it is just the opposite. It is the stepping point through which one may move into the infinite and omnipresent through experience.

This is why it is called an initiation. The initiation is by itself meaningless. It is the passageway or doorway to the infinite and unlimited divine. It is not the end but the beginning, which is its intended purpose. It has a goal. That goal is to awaken the reader to walk through the message to witness the Universal Awareness that leads one to the door of liberation.

We should be so lucky.

There are many elements that are explained in detail in catechism and also in the discourses of the Akshaya Patra Series as we have in the Zanoni Series.

Some things are as stated only "Hints, hints, hints . . ." It is your obligation to discover the rest of it. I cannot do it for you.

- It is not possible to progress in the Universe without [sacrifice]. [Sacrifice] maintains the order of the Universe. Sacrifice pleases the gods; the gods send rain; the rain feeds the crops; the crops yield harvest, the harvest strengthens the limbs and widens the outlook; it

broadens the heart and clarifies the vision until man reaches the goal, where there is no more struggle or death. The highest and the most fruitful sacrifice is that of the ego. Crucify it and be free. Dedicate your ego to God and be rich beyond all dreams . . . —Sai Baba

- The Asu-ra Devata or Pitar-devata (gods) . . . were first Gods [Sura] — and the highest — before they became "no-gods," [Asura] and had from Spirits of Heaven fallen into Spirits of the Earth . . . All these gods and demi-gods are found reborn on earth . . . —Secret Doctrine of HPB

These are the divine intelligences of superconscious energies that incarnate in the creation of life agencies and are born to become the vitality of the material form or mortality.

They inspire what is animate versus inanimate, organic versus inorganic, and are the difference between life and death. The gods incarnate with the breath and also leave with it. The Word lies with the breath and functions through the mind as the superior cause of these.

Their first state is immortality as life energy, and is the difference between the soul, Vital Life Force and the spirit; forming entities that make up the life of Man.

The first state or the God of Being is *satchitananda* or the Being/Consciousness/Bliss as experienced in universal, omnipresent, omniscient: Life, Light and Love.

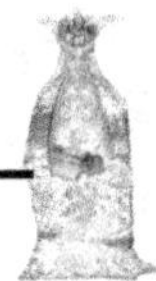

The Original Ceremonial Initiation at AMORC:

[You can see the original play videotaped in Black and White, as presented in 1979 at The Rosicrucian Order, AMORC, in Francis Bacon Auditorium. It was video-taped at a dress rehearsal by Gregg Hungerford.

It was taped without the color emphasis the week before the play was presented: www.vimeo.com/47382759]

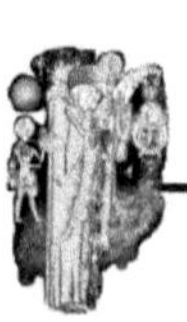

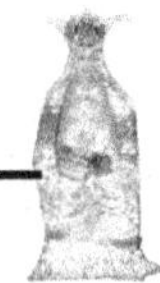

Requiem: Death and Resurrection,

Of Those Seeking Liberation

Life is a pilgrimage to God; the holy spot is there, afar. The road lies right before you; but unless you take the first step forward and follow that step with others, how can you reach it?

Start with courage, faith, joy and steadiness. You are bound to succeed. . .

You know only the present, what is happening before your eyes; you do not know that the present is related to the past and is preparing the course of the future. Each birth wipes out the memory of the one already experienced.

People do not realize that the end of this cycle of birth and death is in their own hands. The tree came from the seed and the seed from the tree . . . since the beginning of time. . .

You claim to have mastered your senses and all low desires, but they sprout at the very first opportunity, just like grass that grows after the first summer shower. . . seek only the Lord and His Glory in Nature. . .

Nature is useful only when it adds to the wonder and awe that it is able to provoke and sustain. . .

Remember, there is nothing in the world which can give you unmixed joy. Even if there is one such thing, when it is lost, you will become very sad!

This is in the very nature of this world. So, try to correct the very source of joy and sorrow, the mind.

On Earth, in our lives, those things of value are placed deep inside the earth. They are hidden purposefully. We are required to seek, to find.

We are not among those planets in the Universe that rain rubies, and have surfaces that are layered in streams of diamonds.

So, forget that alchemy of false generosity. Ours is not so easily shared, purposefully. It is determined by our chivalry.

If we want to reap what is of value, we must go in search. Our quest is our opportunity to discover the things we crave, given the gravity of self-worth.

If we go along and simply pick up everything off the surface of the ground, we will find that we have lived for nothing, but a life of one, whose end is valueless.

Even the seed has no value, unless placed properly in search of nutrients in the earth. So, we dig and discover. That is the true purpose of our initiation.

Otherwise what we pile up is trash in homes that are lived in laziness. These will simply leave us playing like the pauper, when living our lives in that field of recklessness.

We will be seen by friends as someone, who is useless in the end, when true needs of character are to be relied upon for their value, in the nature of self-discovery.

Our fellow man will come determined, knocking to find a friend. But a friend will only come searching for those who have true values in the end.

If Man is so determined as a friend, how much more God, who is in search of the True Devotee, demanding perfection in their

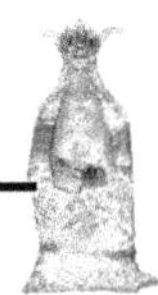

integrity, and nothing less, when questioning.

These values are the true diamonds and rubies. They are those worth possessing of true intelligence.

Not so much those of science, business or political opportunity, but those committed to the Truth when determining the final end.

If questioned when death comes calling, that honesty is undetermined, for seekers seeking answers for, *"Who is God, and who I Am . . ."*

And, that is yet to be determined.

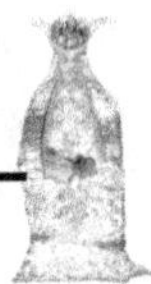

Chapter One

Ha! This parchment is tattered but by its lines it cries,

"Who has come to read my book! Who dares confound me in my nook? Sanctum!"

"Who comes to search and seek? Sanctum!"

"Who to tend the true Mysteries, who comes there to tend the words—comes creeping in the Poets lair? Sanctum!"

"Gods, allied to thoughts entombed come. The resurrection into life, Sanctum!

"Thief! You have robbed the sanctuary. What have you to say for this?

Speak!"

A Whirling Wheel of cloudless Love to spin upon an earthly dream. A thread of cause creates a robed effect, entwining cover, to support the morrow's needs.

This Master Cloak of Cosmic wear is like a vein of gold within the mind. Subtle but prominent. Unseen. Existing.

To share it with lives that it may reap new life, we may be patient, but for what? Another life? Patience came and left in other lives. Where did that patience get us?

So, the pattern is set. We do our best. We live. We care. Masking these powers of inner life. Aware of nothing ourselves, more or less, save by our life and its accomplishments that fade faster than the sunset, before the morning repairs, to break the night, by that solar ray of golden light.

So, we must begin for these are precious times for our beginnings.

We are seeing now, as if by dreaming, visions past the nether

worlds.

The world, past time, delivers us to an ancient graveyard of old composted energies. Atoms now appear, of these once composted lives. We call these back again, to recall their ancient lifetimes.

The winds blow hardly audible with a soft rustling of the trees, as these ancient graveyards come to life, from out of ancient cosmic seas.

Suddenly appearing, these scenes of life sweetly glimmering by imagination, from lighting transferred by invisible agencies—and they shiver now and then.

Now and then . . .

The leaves, faintly seen, clash; shuffling in the outburst of the moving vegetation. It is only quiet seeing without hearing.

Be patient, persevering, we'll get to it, the scenes are coming closer into vision, as their sights are offered up foreseeing the next impression.

The winds brush past the grasses that shake, deflecting shadows with the breeze. These flow erratically, passing through the valley to the world below.

It moves like the curtain; sadly, as a train of ghosts. They are the passing entities flushed red-rosy cheeked in the breeze, flowing down by their light-filled bodies, to the valleys from the cold heights, coming to take their places for preparing coming scenes.

Only the slightest whistle is heard now through the rushing reeds that rustle in the marsh winds. Their shaking breaks the silence suddenly.

Nothing steady. Just now and then.

Water ripples in the pond nearby that glitters in the moonlight water's breathing by the waves of atmosphere.

There's no one there to witness it. So, it's sad. They say

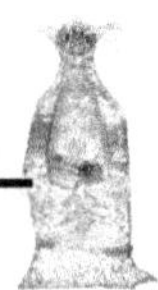

philosophically. It lives without being experienced. Not by Man. Only the One Life that lives in it who is constantly entertained by it.

Soft drumming through the silent space is heard to wake time in the distance, as it pounds the atmosphere. It is far away, but not that far.

Time beating . . .

Their incessant drums are heard always drumming. Time beating time, as the spell is cast. . . Who is here to hear?

Only me.

The village drums beat relentlessly, to pound out the rhythms heard, beside the spirits hum which is ever chanting, in the mind and Archetype.

Native members, they are now constantly wandering, but are gathering together. Come to call together the souls of ancestral spirits, guardians and old watchers from the nether world. They may assist us.

Perhaps they have traveled here by the wind. Perhaps the Atma-sphere, which brings these back by the more-subtle way. They've been traveling beyond the spirit.

They have returned to reach us here. To wait and watch from long distances, traveling by this spirit wind surrounding earth of atmosphere. This to get together here.

Grandfathers and Grandmothers, the ancients, hug close to themselves their treasured relics, of their loved ones as they sit by the sea of energy, recalling their memories of all who have gone before.

Waiting long, they have now come just for this fortunate opportunity.

They pray, "May these all be blessed by the gods glistening, in the

sacred lights of stars at night," sitting silent by the shore.

Their spirits are merging into the elemental atmosphere as they are being called down to council.

The ancient spirit, Time, is being called out to come forward now. We see him.

He comes from the Spirit in the Beginning. He who is most ancient and always first to speak for them in the spirits traveling energies. They sit silent, tongueless, waiting to be entertained.

He appears before us now to open into legends, awakening the imagination in our dream. Supplying our endearment.

And, the soul breathes to conspire with Time to bring us these memories of creations—past conference, brought forth in soliloquy.

Sage Time

Inspiring, I am these captured portions of the personalities to live, inspired by the matter forming stars, and by Time in "I" identity. I alone, appearing in all nativity to mark it with my daydream, am a map before the stars.

Now we shall be tried by our faults by our animated egress into mortality. Our trials infinite. Let the vagrant life begin to fade away. The transgressor shall be heard and their story told and we shall see their lessons for they shall be tried by the conscience and judged by the laws of the invisible by those forces that lie within.

Being witness to the conditions resulting from the daily life. There, the record is kept for future keeping, to draw from that, the path before us.

This is the frequent visit that is inevitable, for I come again and again. You shall be the witness bearing instrument of judgement, as deliverer and executioner, or

the prayer speaking spokesman for your comfort, at the door of entrance, before the path moving forward.

Forget the form. You are not the body! Your evolution shall be perfected by degrees. You decided to be the fool. And Degree work now is the necessity, as the penalty for the conditions imposed by your mortality.

Skill requires you work by degrees in the miracle of Time. And, through initiations by degrees you shall commit to rapid change, to perfection evidentiary as you swear by it to me.

You shall meet and reveal the requirements for lawful re-entrance to the liberation into immortality. Show and demonstrate your character. It shall be required to be worthy of our memory!

Foolish! The pride of inventions, conveniences, and developments. How far shall we fall into these things of evil trash and trinkets that satisfy the senses? How deep the humility to find ourselves the discoverer, to discover our humility as humanity.

How our manners honorably are formed to match the character until we are witness to our true nobility.

These ancient and long forgotten ancestors were peopled planetariums, the witness to the stars. They excelled all processes strengthened out of time. But they are not forgotten save to these modern nations. For those ideals and their idols have appeared at once before me. These were turned down in spirit, in the anguish of insanity born of this modernity.

To those who came before, they brought the prophecies of time and invention, united in the realization of the mystery before the fall.

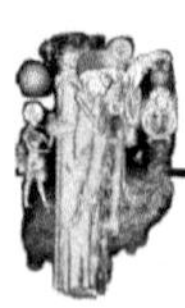

Appearing and creating out of this union of ancient memories, they, in the spirit of the impossible, found the hope for sending forth their light for future nations.

Remembering all, in this invited sight are those once again returning. Lifetime after lifetime, the lack of devotion and the disruption of life in selfish goals have made monarchs transformed into the pauper born—the noble into the ignoble, the saint and sage into the godless form.

Indeed, going back, far back, the fare was paid again and again as the traveler paid the boatman at the river crossing in our initiation, and then as now, it has become paid into extinction.

Recall first what once was by the antique cultural awareness, and acceptance a conscious causation of all that is life, that is only imagined now. Uneducated by temptations, all were scattered witnesses to the being inspired by common sense. Now that is forgotten as if passed on as well into extinction.

Then, go farther back, remember when it was, to think was to know. The realization was an enticement to act— in thought, word and deed; where they lay with a pure heroic heart, and there they were provoked into a moral conscience, and there the desire for that benefit of faith was faithful unto them.

They came, and from those miracles within them, they were fortified by devotion. They charged forward with courage not cowardice, to withstand the fears inflicted by dogmas, false experience and repressions in the truth, for Truth was revealed.

They were challenged. Yes. But they by discrimination left these dark daydreams unexplored by renunciation.

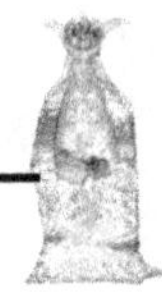

Their knowledge was based upon their union with all nature. They fought with the impossible and as gods in spirit bodies they formed sanctuaries, to become the coalition of the remarkable.

Spirit feeling oneness resigned to serve them, with the Atma-sphere that forewarned them of their fates. They felt the forward rush of time, the flow of the tides, the currents of the Earth and the virtue of her vegetation, and the realization driven by the stars.

No virtue was left covered, as they turned to uncover the desires to know self as "That, I Am That" beyond the elements and the stars.

And from all the galaxies and stars or planets afar that pull was felt; creating demands upon her inhabitants. It was then as it is now, God appearing in human form.

There they gathered in reverent plight, in sacred rites. Where they honored her glory as mathematical spirits and appeared as lighted entities born of time, and there that I, Time, rallied to their causes.

In sacrifice they were able to call forth their spirits from the dead. Recalling worlds upon worlds remembered, as their creative causes united, ruling from within.

But we have now recalled them, and they gather here now—by our will. We have recalled them back, by diligence, trial and test and the applications of the laws of universal causes. They seek our challenge and are born upon the wind and are soon to be appearing.

Their mysteries lie buried here, and they, like angelic predators turned on the Wheel of Time, sit patient for the ready. Waiting on those consumed by serial study and those deserving divine approval. They make appeals and seek a friend forevermore, by this returning empirical

devotion.

How this original culture came to be swept from the face of the Earth, except for those few survivors, we are recalling now.

This is a tale, as legends have it, that shall now be revealed to you. Listen well! We give first our warning. By this discovery, you may be called upon to defend and preserve the Great Laws and Mysteries, and by that knowledge know that we are not alone, where the "Greater than I" have survived to live beyond that death in native form.

That the "I," self-identified, might possess you to know their secrets in Awareness. And, should the "I" be worthy through its sacrifice, become love and faith and service, and by those things performed be bound by duties great. They shall fly away from here soon to her field of liberation. Death and sacrifice are their never-ending Glory.

Our first days are now appearing out of Wisdom endless in self-conceiving, self-created Bra-A-eL-Wau-He-Ya-eeM.

Boundless depth encircling in the orb of orbits bound for its search and pleasure seeking. Reminding us all that we are gods.

Unveil the vast mystery of these seven wonders and their wanderers moving in the dream. These link earth to life's first caused vitality, rising in the column; lit fiery in our mystery of that spirit Kundalini.

Lightning veiled from the beginning is down censored spiraling, spiraled round, like vines winding 'round a Tree, to be formed spherical by its golden mean—Yes, by golden numbers, in Hiranyagarbha the Golden Egg of

Brahma, in golden triads and golden lines, of those lost lineages of golden members and passage of our golden times, and the mysteries of Khan Gu.

There, there the spirals. . . between these twins of Good and Evil—in fires of hot and cold spirits that appear wandering here in spirit, erring to form places in their columns, to stand out for their differences.

Unveil this towered pillar here, within the Central column falling to its depth. Step forward creature, rising to the sun of morning, by way of the God of Victory and Splendor, just to listen.

Thence appearing first ascending with the moon, revealer of the morning, it has peeked above the earth, the Kingdom, from the miracle of Splendor, to the coast of Victory, and thereby we are bound by Beauty, born into greater species, and on to rise to Glory into the invincible principle, seated before that place of liberation. We give honor to our Glory in Chesed.

Now go back and back and slowly back to slumber, ten, nine, eight, seven, six, five, four, three, two, one . . . Begin to reveal the story bit by bit:

Time stops to catch his breath and to contemplate a bit to determine the consequence. After a quiet time, Time begins:

Sage Time (Cont'd)

Beneath the restless rolling seas, the sacred mysteries lie. Lost and forgotten in the outgrowth of the new and less compliant cultures.

With them went the citizens of natural endowments. Beings once given sanctuary, within their thoughts, and mores of sacred origins.

Gone . . . downward cast these landscapes once fell beneath the seas, into graveyard in the deep. Seething in the depths, hot rock broiled, unveiling gases and then cooling, to conceal those mysteries!

Immortal days now unfold our spirits imagery, in our first steps, moving into subtle Splendor. Bound, by the burden of mortality, we inspire moral destiny without delay.

Hurry! Before the time sets, and the ideal time has lost its light moiré, for revealing this mirrored reality of the Ancient Lord of Days.

The impatient foot first stepped into tender energies with each impatient step. The misguided soul steps forward, now inspired for transformation, unto Victory, and faces on to Glory from above in that far distance.

Step . . . Step now. Outnumbered, by all creatures on our way. They point out our defects, as the candidate moves passing by all these members standing by, hearing endless accusations.

Your will has limitations that are waking to the taking of that way.

These, by days, are timed to lunar motion, as if musically inclined, to forces trafficking through space, and the happiness or misery of spirits fortunes, for things acquired or denied.

You are free, decide! Pick your time. Pick your place of destination.

The Guardian waits beyond the gates. First stepped in the sphere of perfect destiny.

Last days will be lasting days, if deemed Eternity. For they are purchased by one's everlasting virtues before seating in immortality. As those seen seated in the far

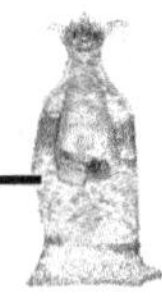

distant along the way have done before.

We inspire and aspire to fulfill these cycles of our days, and these are days first formed for our lifetimes of renewing energy. We, cycled for good or wasted memories, are first weighed by the heart, with each passing moment of our destined memories.

Waking working days' pass preparing our initiation. For waking in the spirit.

We moronic, run quickly; passing through mortality, as drunkards on a binge. Waking in our dream.

There are these lifetimes awaiting that we must contend with to get beyond all this.

We search around. More-vast they, the ancient native members of time-creatures huddling. Genius members seen discerning periods of time. By the looks on faces they are perfect in their slumbers—Timed creatures perfect placed.

More of these members stare out seeing, than the lonely eves and mornings, but they play in day and night dreams. Do they mention Time as the mirror of our stars—the gods above us in the suns, are there to test our vows. Lighting up the darkness. They are spirits of intelligence.

They are now standing fast nearby, staring into moiré patterns that shine along with those shadows on our walk across the sky.

They formed their stations. They peak at midday and midnight. And they become as webbing written in the starlight far beyond our space and time.

We are fortunate to pass. But, we have no choice in this.

They are lives that are living immortality. They are

seated in vast numbers. Stationed according to their times.

They are the unimaginable witnesses, though we may speak to them, to measure time, they project into our secrets there and never move from their places.

Secrets in our prayers are also sent, and by these we are drawn to those spirits, who live beyond the atmosphere, in the place of Atma-sphere.

Where are those who once traveled east and west? Where are those citizens? They slumber now, somnambulistic, waiting on our reminiscences. We will call them back.

Mu, the once-was, is now quietly remembered by its old and silent thoughts. Those slumber dreaming in a sea that is pacific. Nothing stirs in its silence. Silent Mu. We wake the sleeping embers of those ancient reminiscences, by invoking our myth-memory out of these.

We see before the dawn, daylight reappearing somewhere, as those appearing faces of those who once were remembered well. We hear their canticles; as sung by their forgotten ancient songs.

Songs are heard, across grass surfaces once danced, and whereon they traveled peacefully, for purposing. Recalling now those born of mysteries they in turn hear my request. They are calling back. Together, we are celebrating Time, for I am the ritual made sacred to any time, and I awaken those who sleep in omniscience.

My image ever-living shines, reflecting the moral image. "I Am, Eyeh Asher Eyeh."

The stars in their gapped spaces in Atma-Sphere delight

that canopy of night. We still see the stars moving in their places. But my moving is that love that is written into breath.

"I Am" hidden and everlasting righteousness. Now, we witness stillness in the stars. Sparking, they shine a little brighter as we move time backward in our storyline.

My fires lightly lit come from old lives of fiery embers, sparks remaining of that inner fire—chirping, breaking crackling members.

They become vehicles conspired to call out native lights. They come together to gather vacant minds and call the spirits of the night.

Heavens hear us shouting, "Shamayim! Shamayim!"

Shem-Sham the bliss of happy names on Mayam-Mayim as the goddess Miri-yam, the Mother's waters, reflecting that light of Light.

Forces move by the sound as a cloud waving and streaming, orbiting and animating. We are their mirror reflecting spirits. An aura witnessing new life. The reflection of that illuminating mind is now seeing everywhere. Its spirit space and time.

We are Time. Laughing? Damned, are the souls recalled, and they witness to foresee their future returning to the past, and reaching back into mortality on the Tree of Life.

We are here unmasking immortality in our moral daydream. We call:

"Come back waking-sleeping."

Come back? They must come back. I have called them. I Am. There are no free choices here.

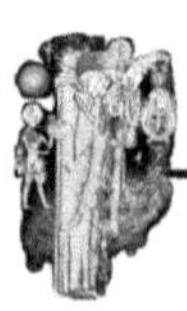

Where imagination thinks, fools exist, knowing nothing! The nothing knowing, we know these. They are among those who are called back to us from these dreams as well.

"Bring back those Mysteries."

Where are they? Gone are the mysteries! Beguiled by the hands of time, and consumed by the lascivious vulture of mortality. They are swallowed into immorality. They are as feeding carrion.

Who has eaten the fruit of that tradition? The Beast Severity. Who has eaten the fruit of good and evil? Who eats to devour the filth of vulgar generations who pass away in death? Severity.

Delight. It is to be for the Love-born yet. These near waking are only demons all, though human love may live in them as divine. Who wakes to our mortality again? These same friends and neighbors.

The God of Love will live in them. These no more than ancient puppet dolls.

There seen, appearing in our daydreams, they come in our imagination. There are also some creatures called Divines.

Walking in spirit-air. Breathing, before formation, they all are coming as to a jealous feasting.

They come o'er the valley of death, until waking here repeating and repenting, "I am becoming Man and man again," as their soul's march, descending to our destination.

As a bird in migration, each soul comes returning, to feast upon what is truly death. After leaving the form they are recalled back to live carrion.

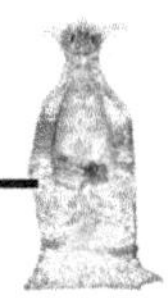

There comes the soul's feasting. It is an ideal inheritance, from long-forgotten generations, now returning to reap their karmic tithes.

Side-by-side those old who are lacking memories, their false desires are recalled, or those waking who are now facing their forbidden actions—they arise to mourning since we have disturbed their waking-sleeping. Reborn they return to that world of worn out forgetfulness.

Our thoughts prevail when they are waking. Be at peace! They remember false discriminations. Shocking mortality. There are those coming who have forgotten our art of medicine, for living in mortality. They forgot those mortal lives that were lived in those accidents, plagues and diseases. They come now to relive these with the conscience voiced doctors, and those who eat poured out prescriptions. They are returning once again with those who died on battlefields.

Selfish desires turned back long ago. Once again are called, to relive their temptations of emptiness, to be pleased again at the touch of mere sensation, that are misleading those to death and desecration. They each follow one another, some who were smiling first and not so keen when reminiscing.

We must be reborn again to do this memory. For this life to be relived, to fast long upon the daydream, in this our vigil of initiation.

Thereby we may see if our lessons that were learned one minute each, in moments at a time, are still recalled.

"Look back!"

Deep recalling now those memories. Our lives regressing, going back into those pasts portending.

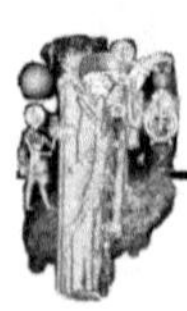

We retell stories never told out loud. This recalls our false history. Bearing the insult of regrets for long lived forgotten memories.

And worse, some lives that were perhaps unforgivable. Sad.

But from the Ancient Generation that Golden Age of wonder calls us back to remember. It is time to clear the way. That precious knowledge lost, it calls us by its saying,

"Bring back the memory!"

With the history of our ancestors vanished, but not gone away! We are here to witness, and return to face ourselves for the coming Golden Age.

Purify your hearts with that. Find your peace! Clarify your minds to witness what has vanished! Recall those days of ancient sages. Recall those sacred lands that once housed beloved shores that now have disappeared.

Those lands once torn asunder and swept by the tides—those swallowed by the seas and reduced to ancient memories. Call back the Time forgotten, and those we lost, friends and families, of those time forgotten entities? Those defeated . . . as the world retreated, long before the fall of that ancient mystery, on the ancient Tree of our ancestry.

Vanquished by that miracle! Albeit the misfortunate, the hapless, wretched, pitiful, and those all deserving of our pious pity. Send your prayers for one another on your return.

Recall those elements that formed them, and demand their return to us. We want those bones, half hidden. Those old bones once buried by the sands beneath the

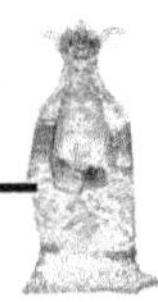

ocean floor.

Worn by the formidable influence of Earthly custody these bones are penalties for Wisdom's death and for your coming into this Age without clearing up the debt. All have been worn away, but they are now recalled to be forgiven.

In the depths of time there lie those buried bones of all past memories. Memory must be freed of all regret. The Being, that dark custodian of Earth, who has swallowed this.

In those ancient days, they assembled in their cultures, where they passed peacefully. We recall those denizens; whose morals were beyond deference.

But jealous, these fatal eyes of mine have been watching over them. These jealous bones of theirs are mine to be remembered. They were painted by my reckless art of transforming energy. By skills pulled up from graveyards they are rewritten, as if by my unkind artist's hand. If they have been abused by them, they must be made correct.

Knowledge, if remembered, is the defender of our lost infancies. But we forget. Wisdom is plagued by deceit since it believes in honesty.

Past lives passing are repeatedly born back into Time. They are vagabonds repeating lives that should have been unrepeatable. Following their destinies to relive their nakedness, due to that lived, and not that determined by me. My determinations were simple. By their actions alone, these were complicated.

They forever pass through Me, passing by me. For I Am Time, but I did not recall them. They were created by me and therefore they became my custody. I am innocent,

living in these timeless days, and though bedding down repeatedly, they bed down here, tied in their own bridled binding ways.

In their mortal stables of flesh and bone, they returned as animals. Unable to get set free in liberation, they are recalled. This was not me, but continues 'til death entreats them, they wander once again, nakedly, until they have perfected this.

Visceral Man, living like those half-animals, forgetful of their once transparency, seeking death in flesh only, seeking the ends in their mortality. These fools are witnessed as those forming recovering humanity.

To be recalled to a feasting? Yes, by ignorance eating by their labors. False tables are set by these devourers. For these are saints turned into creatures, built of peat, mineral, salt and stone.

There remain only those lies of false appearances, Maya-Mayim, the watery illusion. They are the wavelets remembered here for us for setting up our staging.

It is not for me complaining, but recall, bodily remnants of sacred denizens, the garment of their appearances in those forgotten cultures now forebode in our morose remembrances.

Once these people were scattered wide across the world before collapsing. They never intended to be defeated, and some escaped their beloved shores. But, they lost their memory, forgotten through the ages.

I stand with you, for you, who have come here, who are parcels made of this. Poor vagrants, unable, with your speech and mouth to speak for you are forgetful. I will hold you to your memory, and will risk your extortion, as one confined to misery. Saying first this, because I am

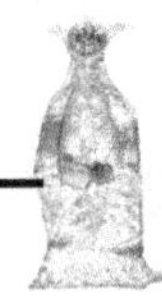

the old, "I-Am-Time" and only ask that you please,

"Remember Me."

Burden bound, by laws and principles. Live, to regret inevitably, your lives lived, before the passions of your Lord. I curse the day that you were born. That day is darkness. God may not regard it truly by night, and no light may shine on its form, for it is Glory by the day.

The floral shades from the Valley of the Shadow of Death may stain it. And in sorrows it is cultivated. No song or joyful voice can sound it. The dirge is elegy to rise against the curses of the day. This from the time of ancient mourning. For death is all that is remembered, for these ages passing by the Lord of Providence.

So, let the stars be dark and forgetful. They need not turn away. They may not look on these forgetful souls who wander, in the world of misery, for having kept the tomb and womb. Others are waiting at the doorway, for walking into sad memories.

They may all be the flesh again, inspired by the ghosts who wake within the bellies. They come before the Mother's pleading. These flesh mothers are their members, birthing in the world. She gave birth to forms of wonder, by gods rendered perfect in the womb.

Oh regret!

What gold may buy, it cannot buy relief. What was, is gone, when death passed by unrepentant, it came forgetful with our hour from birth seeking life and death. Knowing lives lived are just a moments monument.

I have taken up the score count many times, and left behind these lives unfulfilled, but I have been trying to fulfill them.

These creatures besting deaths appearing only shades of men, who by better lives, are sometimes seen overcoming death. They were the liberated living who lived on, while deaths came for others regardless. Leaving behind, only desolation with no cause for sacred places, for their burials to be remembered. They came, but they didn't die.

These long-lived free and liberated by Gold medicines, followed those who returned as dumbed intrusions into leading dying lives. While those dead living were darkened more by making up their academic lies. So, these saints stayed on assisting those who think and speak before they know. Now they wander in their shadows.

How do we deal with all of them?

Weary days. For the weary dying, whose days are filled with fear for that moment of the grave. Gold and Silver may not cause their return again. There's not enough to feed them.

As that ancient land of the everlasting, Mu, crushed beneath the seas, recall now those witnessed in their sacred memories, and forgive those poor members who lost their souls to merge back to immortality. Leaving those fair mortals who were lesser, far behind, to live false lives in beggary.

They have left those false-faced behind to deal with this alone. But they hint! O' hint! O' hint!

"Hint, hint, hint...!"

We've had enough of hints. Where did it get us?

Some escaped the fate of those descending deeper, falling into forms. They surrounded themselves in purity, beside the Kingdom of the Lord.

Some, like droppings became like those fallen leaves in autumn. They were scattered, unremembered. With them, the winter fell and then the cold. They left decomposed. While their faithful' left behind were trapped, caught helpless by nature's hold.

Living things. All of these. Cultivating lives, their fear rushing into that wilderness went below again and again, to burn their flesh in deserts, or chasing through the jungles, they hid in safety by wrapping in their foliage or coverings in sand.

Naked. Flesh torn. They stood aghast against death. They lived to face the frightful entity for the long road ahead. Such were days turned into ages.

World, worlds and worlds surrounded and covered them in death and dismemberment—banished, death challenged, starved in senses.

Daily death, diseased and this before facing wild creatures and the elements? Heaven is hell composting in this graveyard!

Burn this flesh to dust and ash, when the fellow's dead! Recall again by my hour hand. For every act returns again.

The more fatal death blows came by reaching for one's inner enemies and then enjoying them. Death as life came and went by the gate into the world alone.

Creatures were happy to live unhappy, sharing in their wilderness and fighting with their jealousies. Their enemies. Intemperance, jealousies, envies and the worlds of indifference in that animal man. Political intrigues. Lies, lies and more lies!

But I am not complaining.

The false-faced face facing forward moving untoward toward the truth. Before the sun, they stand waiting now for their initiation.

There they stand, and I to greet them with their lies saying, "This is my body." False. "This is my blood." False. For these belonged to nature and I created them. False witnesses. My ears are shattered. Before those members who do not know, and yet they come to ask peace of me.

Vagrants, come again to realize the wisdom of the self. They were temporary travelers, buried in a leather bag. Where are those old false-faced demons now? Are they good or do they lie? For liars love to lie and call it cleverness. Where is wisdom? Virtue's ingrates living lives regretful, must answer for it. They seek shelter in recall of me, but fearing life lived for false-morality, they are the false-lovers who have died, repeatedly. How long does this go on?

Unjustly they smartly-ignorant scoff. We are mocked by their dull geniuses. Forget this world of false memory, decide to forget the dream and sink into the past, to discover that mystery in that once sacred sanctuary of the Golden Age of Mu, before going farther back.

We must now invoke our past to recall it. To evoke its ancient memory of that Golden Age. Recall the vision from those long-forgotten shores and the sacred lives, once loved, of ancient memories.

Now softly . . . Be at peace Pacifica! O' ocean. We will call that ground to swell once again. Where that peaceful sea rolls in the majestic sweep over many thousands of miles. There dwelt that vast continent of Mu. In purpose, subtle as the subtle entity. Righteous unto the good cause, as the life brought forth from the Immortal

Entity. Subtle energy born of superconsciousness in that subtle state, before all came to live in this unhappiness.

Far gone and lost, our garden . . . from those subtle Golden Days that lived in sunlit minds, and the peace inspired by the Lords of immortality.

What was near once, is now far away and that is sitting there buried. Buried deep beneath the Earth far below the sea.

Her people passed in those past and long forgotten days. They were recipients of peace, from the dawn of light. Descended from the immaculate who came into a world that was Time ordered, being shaped into these mortal geometries, that formed bodies in the flesh from clay— being greeted and arrested by these new masters who became the cause of disease and death and avarice.

The earth condensed, and concentrated down that flesh condemned into the matter born. There came these with the breach of trust, as brackish denizens, formed as salting seas covered in mortality, encrusted as if becoming new garments made with mineral ornaments.

In alchemical laboratories, the bowels appeared, and there these new organs formed. To breach those contracts with the spirit entity they fell into my form.

We break it here! Sworn enemies of our memories. As enemies forgotten these are also now recalling. You ate the flesh of animals and plants, and now you are the cause of it. The desire is amplified in sensual appetite.

Through the daylight hours now moving toward divinity, we are on this path of initiation and that from out of darkness into light. Each passing thought, hour by hour, day by day, becoming wasted into the weeks and months and years unending, the upward path returning by these

initiations that are awarded to us, who pass with moral destinies—one good deed at a time, returning from mortal blackness to walk out of darkened night.

> *"O' Light, O' Light, O' Light,*
> *I am thy Beauty Bright!*
> *Juliet, Jovial and Jolly."*

All lives were supported by the laws, rules and principles, in the magic of her initiations. All came and went as if by changing dress, with old garments washed, and then gone, returned again—dunces awakened lifetimes after lifetimes.

All forgot, but they were not forgotten—not by me, the first-born. For "I-Am-Time, the never sleeping."

Bodies lay discarded along the path of destiny. Graveyards thereby renewed again. Supported by the Spirit of the Motherland, they slept before the sea washed these all away. Remembering those who fought long, saddened in the end, on the path of her initiation. They were cast into what seemed doomed from the beginning.

Ancient races now extinct. We are now recalling and in that spirit, they are awakened, from their days of dreaming.

You are not the body. You are not the mind! You are born from innocence as the bodiless, endless time—like the pearl in the ocean, as spirit round, but with a face, before the substance formed.

Your cultures, your monarchies, your civilizations were mastered as a sacred initiation. They are gone, but now the memories are returning.

Your initiations shine as embers now fanning into

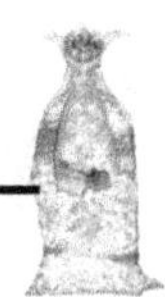

flame—broadcasting my nature. For I Am Time. My fire, my embers, are revealing past and future nations, ritualizing light.

Unmasking ancient friends and angels to be the prodigals of dreams. Your tests have been that witnessed. Mine with yours and yours with me, in time. Immortalized, appearing out of darkness into light.

What has become of your ancient nation? Now here recalled again.

You were then, now. Being—united in one thought, there formed and conceived within a magical center you transformed into the outward entity.

Your spirit outward turning, turned unwound, where two worlds converged, colliding above and below, in and out, the subtle to the gross, and together the heavens and earth united, midway up, to climb the Tree of Life.

Where is that playground now in this moment? Rising up into that subtle Atma-sphere. You are not the body nor the many bodies!

Creation formed and changed form again, and turned by the outward motion—unwinding, spun to shine thru reflection in one nature. Intended first in this motion. You became their denizen, the poor sad citizen, and then departed, only to return again.

Declaring your standing with ego on returning worse than when it left. As if you had mastered it. You stood before the Everlasting, bleating voiced, as the lamb, as the one stooping between heaven and earth. You, contrasting the invisible and visible. There you were suddenly standing as an ungrateful animal—unreformed as the dark entity without a memory pleading, as if a worthy candidate. You, nothing more than the sperm of

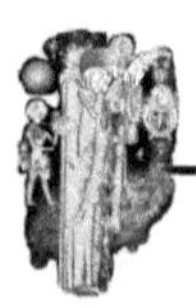

reform, and making demands on me.

There, the spit of Spirit. Fallen into the field of matter born—begging for earth and ash to eat, becoming mineral, clay and peat.

It breathes at least. Pumping and pounding hearts like these drums beating in the distance. Where time is ever played until old age, when it is finally ringing in the ears.

In one consciousness, that world revealed the vital powers encircling earth. These became our futile vital states.

In rapture, it established you, the personality. And with that the theater of character which we can measure, by square and compass, in the primal mystery of life.

It clearly walks. It talks incessantly. The Word incarnated into the mind, and the superior form appeared, in this matter born. Therein the spirit trapped itself. By self-confining it transforms its inner life in immortal mortality born.

The light, inspiring suddenly, in a moment of refreshment, the mystery begs now for that power of hidden meaning—and by the letters, numbers and powers symbolized, they become by these idols born. Where we were hidden once, in the attributes of light and life? We are now recalled to the spirits revealing form.

O' happy life. Here, we are in need to be revealed again. So, we meet in our daydream together finally. Are you happy now? Here, in this abstract form of things unknown? Here, we have become their letters, their numbered features and abstractions. They are just replacements and substitutions, sharing space with each new meaning, in the sea of vacuums on this world of subtle form.

We, in the dream image of these mantric emblems are here rehabilitated, where space and time are transformed by superconsciousness, passing between the spirit and the form. We form their alchemy and revel in their wonder. Happy, happy, happy days, but only for a moment. Our pessimism is anxious though we pretend our endless patience.

What a mystery. Time, Space and Consciousness, they were in supreme cause, transformed into us as bliss, and the happy state of superconsciousness. We are the Logos entity. Shall we dance with glee, or will tomorrow be just another day of your longstanding misery.

Name and Form, we are that inspired onto the surface of the world.

There, now, the East breaks. Juliet or Julius the sun rises to remind us, as a thing to serve us, by its vibration torn from elements, and molded by their minds, that we are in cycles and by this filled with their vibrancy. Each daily witnessed more and more—appearing, in this, as our rightful divinity.

I have turned time around. I Am That. I can do that. I peer into the wonders of the inevitable. You are again fortunate. How? That I even talk to you.

People once were governed, under the soul's benediction in the Kingdom of the Motherland, by Sun and Moon and Mother.

Fair Mu, fair Lemuria. For from her came the consciousness forming into the many races, and by that in voice, we wasted time and became the babel-born.

So, may we now return? No! We are not finished. Look! There, even now. By this first word and you retreated!

Lazy, I am thinking and still confessing and you will not have heard the last of it, so listen.

From out of the earth, before mundane contractions, the babe newborn. The form, established in new life, raised itself into animate genders.

Loving God, love God and they came first form of earth as before, and they in their generations followed, deaf, dumb and blind; each generation out of the womb from the beginning.

The world of intelligence is filled with these scripted in their nonsense. Who is greater than the other?

Silence. The captured species of life is charmed into being. You appeared and it dreamed and I have captured it. Why tell the secret of the beginning?

The Guardian of Reason is caught creating life spontaneously. Quiet!

You, there, dumb animal, given a dominion, under the subjection of this spirit, you became the earthly children, in the sperm of generation. Your old age will find you out, as nothing more than dumb animal otherwise. So first learn to listen. Or, leave.

A set of moral standards are awakened as the deed of righteousness is written, to give place to ethical consideration. Quiet! Stop the mind from thinking.

Out of Nothing, the Ancient of Days from the ancient ring of light, set about the task of recalling back the forgotten generation. It released upon the world its life form, as the pre-existent infinity, and it became the Avatar of God.

There in those special days, the soul of immortality sent upon the earth that ray of truth, to live out the daydream

with us, as the primal cause existence. The Avatar of God came as daylight dressing into night to walk among us graciously.

These forms of man considered there and then a changed humanity—day by day from youth to gentry into old age. They formed then and there. Regenerative powers and conceptive forces came to life, and became the firstborn wonders of God, in universal form.

The spirit of the Word was born. The sage as a universal form, came and stood in the same line with those following through in initiation. One by one their days passed by, and they were the delight of ancient civilizations. They came back one by one, again and again to release their prodigals until no one listened.

The Creator-Preserver divided and multiplied as the animating principle and there the Spirit Man was born, and in spirit the Avatar was reborn again, in the form of the celestial potential and microcosmic form. Ash to ash each moment and dust to dust, this was hardly inevitable.

Twins of spirit. Flesh unrevealing, in good and evil rivalry, it is now time to recall you back to the beginning. No more reminiscing.

Upon every field, wild and wonderful, life giving fruit formed symbols of her transfiguration, the earth was born as would be the paradise of composting entities.

On fields, the herbs and grains grown fragrant by their floral talismans. Appearing in their fragrance we take in these. Their might inspired by the blooming atmosphere, and by their seeds blown traveling into wind they replenish those before them.

They are planted here. And upon the feast of these the

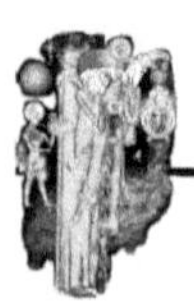

races fed, and found delight in our imagination.

But we should not return here forever more. We should seek our liberation. These inspired fed the Sons of Wisdom, as the Magic in happiness by their sacred spirits. They formed in the magic of daylight in their delight.

They assumed the infinite, invisible Being as an abyss of darkness from the beginning.

Pray! Those days became the numbered and they became outnumbered by infinities that stood by in the heavens for them.

First caused creatures, animals and Man in their spirit generation were tested day by day, and were witnesses to the Love of Wisdom in philosophy. These were once silent and relentless. The mockery of the Lord.

Unable to remain inactive, the invisible diffused in emanations, and decreased within its nature, in sense perfection the farther removed, and they descended into more and more the finite form.

Each by each ascended once again. Alone. As the wanderer who fled to live with strangers, but is now returned again.

They came as creatures who were by women born. Those gods became men of form, perfect geometries, but by the goddess in her beauty they were reformed.

We recall them now. One sound uttered in silence. Coming to this from that nothingness. We return. We are the symbol of our evermore, installed by the primitive rite of life.

From two sounds, they now are formed as One, that we may rise, as the heavens and earth unite. Rushing

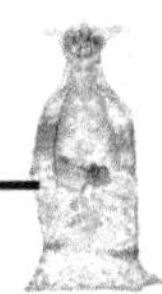

streams cascading meet, and whirling in the whirlpool portending freely greet, into what's become the pool of life, and thought, as light illuminating light.

The two worlds colliding now divide as the good and evil ignite, as the fire touched to dry tinder reacts by spitting water out.

One consciousness forms through our meditation and the lightning from out of concentrations. The yoke unwrapped off the neck, by that noose loosened around all members.

Time is faithful. Time is sworn. One life thereby is reflected shining as the universal light, alive inspired once again in animate beings born.

Bound in One earth as the One inspired, alight, take up the bed and follow me. United, in the bonds of One thought, all gather in One common observance. We are appearing now as promised perpetuating her rites and meanings, to celebrate beneath the starlight and pass into her wonder.

One Life, One Light, One Love, omniscient and excitable. I am again that promise, to bring you back again to the three-fold infinity. Where here you are reformed by the Skilled Workman, and by demiurge. We are united by the voiced action of the egregore. Our treaty is in treatment fair.

Reveal! From out of the cradle of water and fire comes the first thoughts of our creation.

Here! Awaken! We hear it calling us deep, deep into the sea. We answer back as the mind reaches out into perpetual time! And the drums invoke her memory!

Drums fade into twilight. The Sea of Death sits not far out to sea,

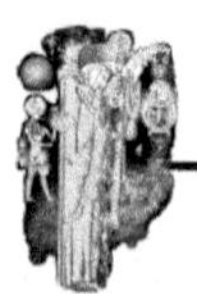

where fire and water meet, and there their forces spit their formations of rocks hot hissing, pelting, breaking and collecting; not far from the peaceful shores unseen.

The continents are becoming stiff in condensation, and the tidal shifts part in celebration of changes that are forced by weathering, as magnetic fields are changing, weakening and strengthening as they are fluctuating, in their new regeneration—and by the seas relentless pummeling that will shortly break away.

There the mountains begin to rise with some early peaking from the sea. It has taken time to spin into a new regeneration, determined by the field and the distance from the sun, as the axis is near to flipping and the world turned upside down.

There is revealed the unsteady lands that are also breaking away and retreating, and there is a vision of an unsupportive hand at play.

The continent is shifting and the fields of form beneath the feet desire to shake in their attempts to break away.

Some plain fields pressured ascend that are loosened, and others descend, or those pressures that are still to be released, and by their parting are near breaking, and some are pushed to slowly separating by their softness in retreat.

The Mystery Words of God coughed up to aggravation that has turned the numbers inside out and upside down, by their labor.

And, with these movements they will soon lose the joy, of all the ancient generations, as their continent falls away, and the world turns upside down, turning darkness into daylight and lights once day to darkness gone away, with the changes in their state. World flipping.

As day turns into night and their nights turn into day, their new proximation discovered, breaks in the old-world order, changing all as these their ancient mysteries fade.

Chapter Two

Sound is heard playing in the autumn air. The sea shifts to broad waves rolling wide, deep and long. Three people come walking out of the waters. They part the sea where they pass.

As they approach dry land they are transformed into solid shapes of living flesh and blood. Buildings appear out of thin air and these become filled with lab assistants, as they begin working within structures not far from the sea.

Solei walks out of solar atmosphere; her garments are flowing witness to her spirit entity—Her beauty surpassing Beauty. She is the Diana likened to all these, gentle as the goddess she appears to be, out of dark mythological concealment of that once living mystery.

 This lab appears to be the lab of many wonders. She is the Beloved. She is the assistant to the director when working next to Paris.

She passes by one lab assistant who works on a crystallization process consisting of a bowl of milky fluid. Beneath the bowl three lights flare in yellow, cyan and magenta sweetly glowing and with its changing it gives off a smell, sweet, as if that daylight were driving the floral fragrance. And there are lights appearing and disappearing that are transforming shapes and densities. In these are orbital clouds and they appear as faces, appearing in a mirror.

The assistant has light conversation as Solei moves on to another assistant silently at work, engrossed in her processes and inattentive to the rest. This second one is working on large crystalline methods that live in heavy lifting liquids that sit in closed glass-like crystallite containers. She is working on a metallic stone, and so she must watch with patience the

temperatures in metal fermentation, working attentively watching for a gaseous transformation and their sudden change in color, as the oils within are grown from nothing.

These gaseous spirits are captured as if the drops had a life of their own. Their perfumes fill the atmosphere if escaping and cannot be recovered ever-more. So she watches to ensure their capture is maintained in their closures containment.

With a word, the assistant lifts some of these shapes, that are from the self-formed living creatures of stone but are very delicate, and she begins attaching one to the other magnetically as an energy property of the oil. The oily properties cause foamlike suspensions in space, that are semitransparent as the form is fashioned into a shape, as the model of atmosphere, yet these shapes appear to take the profile of their image concentrations, being live and pliable by nothing but the mind. They are neither material nor immaterial, but are a starry metallic substance of the mind.

Solei watches to ensure she makes no mistakes. Then the crystal is suspended in air spinning, and she causes it to spin and rotate as a sphere, rapidly. It glows suddenly red while it spins into a globe.

In this process, the inner superfluid metallic oils spread through its subtle subzero gravity thicknesses equally. The mineral shaped properties of this metallic atmosphere, form a container as a spinning solid in gaseous-liquid state. This is shaped of nothing more, than translucent lattice states that are shaped magnetically from the properties of the mass of semi-metal liquids, created by the transformation of oils in their extremely pure and subtle atmosphere, and this is combined with a strange airy powder of metals.

After sufficient fermentations and coagulations, they are created into a single property in ultra-purity, while in a vacuum, and they are combined in subzero state temperatures in a zero-gravity place.

This exposes various characteristics of divinity that are absolute and intelligently reactive in its mass, and this gives it pliability and intelligent properties. It would be completely invisible save for its interior oily state.

Solei then moves on to the final assistant who works with a miniature vessel that glows red as the first, and has a cloud that forms around it.

Concluding, Solei steps into the center of these three assistants, and then makes calculations and measurements as she looks around and waits. She uses her instruments lifted in the light to see. She then keeps a steady eye on every process taking place.

Quiet! All sound ceases as if silence walks in space, with the presence of Paris, as he makes his entrance out of pure energies.

Assistants conclude. They quickly shut down their processes or suspend their works in animation, in a steady state. They stand at attention, and then leave upon Solei's confirmation.

She waves them off, as if what is in the works has a secret that is delicate. All depart to give Paris and Solei their private space.

Paris

Beloved Solei! Your thoughts are even now confided in moral virtues of secrecy, yet their voices have been calling me. I have come.

Though it appears Sage Time has tricked us into this. Though I know not how and my thoughts and memories are foggy.

Sage Time has here amassed a cloud of witness to wake us to the spirit of truth, and by this it has brought us out, troubled by our-past memory, to relive these events in our ancient lives.

Sage Time has placed us in the path of our ancient

virtues, and we relive what was once written into our ancient characters, by their lettered laws.

This scene. . .

I am confused. With our lives here appearing, has appeared out of nothing, and we are burdened, brought here by this—and now, we are realizing this once again, by our ancient sentient labors.

How?

We may be as suddenly lapsing into forgetfulness as we conclude, forming into this great condensation miracle.

Behold, here displayed are the fruits of our ancient accomplishments before us, and these from our once loved ancient labors.

These things engineered are placed before us once again, but I fear as before, they will not see their day, as I am suddenly forgetting faster than I remember, but I sense and relive the past with those regrets.

The earth is shaking once again, and it wakes us slowly while we sleep and dream.

What is happening?

Ignorance abhors light and desires to destroy that which makes it uncomfortable, and memories thereby behold it as our weakness, in this miracle beyond our control.

The ugliness of its dark immorality is concealed, even when disguised in arguments, for this dream of divine uncertainty is burdened by the earth.

How did we get here? We have appeared as in a dream.

The Kingdom of the Motherland's genius, Sage Time, has evoked our play, and so we have come to relive this as we should.

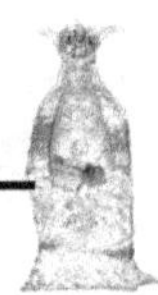

Our desire, now is to unfold the ancient moments and those monuments of regret. With each breath, we are returning to the moments of their memory.

The politics is in season. I have seen beyond our world into that other world of mortality far below us. Great financial wealth is to be had by those amassing vehicles of power in great numbers.

They have begun to live by selfish measures, though worse in Kali Yug. They control the people by their tactics of fear and commitments to their false faith, taking what is unknown to them, by that scattered everywhere, but heard in the confusions within their memories. They chase after the fear of their imagination.

They are manipulated by their demons who take their pleasures, in order to control the people, the political and family life, true values, morality and philosophies.

They are dead to the gods and their labors.

Their world is troubled by its selfish interests, and we are about to lose our safe place in the world of happiness— subject here to dwell within the middle place. Perhaps we may be aided, if we can get away.

For I fear, dear Solei, we are standing once again where that fall is immanent.

He holds up a long box as if that has as suddenly appeared, and with it he enters into forgetfulness.

Solei stares in compassion attempting to listen, but by the transference of thoughts, she feels withdrawn from his voice, as all that was spoken has entered into silence.

Her amazement lists, as she relives her life of that forgotten memory. The box contains an instrument of self-control that he is now revealing.

Paris (Cont'd)

Peace. From all the Gods, there is cherished no greater reward, my sweet.

Solei

Does counsel provide my peace?

Paris

(lovingly)

No, no counsel. But perhaps a new thought inspired in this. Here, see what I have brought . . .

He unveils their Rod of Eltron and lifts it reverently in fond adoration. Stones glitter as if lit by daylight. They live as if given life by art and imagination. The stones each sharing their atomic power.

Paris (Cont'd)

Done! This work. Our thoughts concealed in these Stones of Eltron . . .born from MaSh-Mak Ashtar-Vidya, in the death and resurrection of the Tau center of the Lord Asar's Ea-ST-eR, to expose the Sidereal Forces of element motion in the intro-atomic fields, of the subtle entity.

Beyond the dynamic form of the gods, as found around the pre-elemental stars and gaseous planets, of extreme magnetic fields and gravity. Where God is found as the great and powerful energy, in the early stage of pre-existence.

The cloud penman, in the Eye of Mind, is exposed and we examine every letter for the cloud of creatures that are in them. We are called by the Royal Ribhus to transform

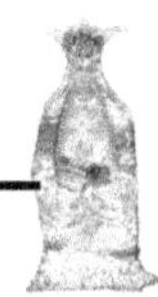

these grand elements of the Golden Abhraka stone of De-Baurah.

We have seen these stones performed in the great laboratories of the gods, as we assumed their nature's in the great stars, planets and moons.

We have seen these with our inner eyes, revealed plainly in the Atma-sphere, when projecting into their stars. These great creatures appear, as they are revealed and communicating between them to us, from their divine intelligences.

Ra-Zi-El the first light formed spirit of alchemy, has spread these throughout creation, in the great Golden Egg center of Bra-Hath-Shyam.

They are controlled in great vacuums and by gas-phase lightnings they are formed. In their chambers of violent storm reactions, within their alchemical world-globe based sepulchers, of superconscious energies surrounding nearby stars, we evoke them.

This staff lives in my thought, by these methods of jeweled creatures, that we have created.

They are the transformed as the Chin-Ta-Mani metal stones from plasmic elements, or the Tattuvanyani kal.

They behave as if omnipotent, omniscient and omnipresent deities.

They were created in exceeding cold and under pressures that are unbelievable. They formed in our pyramids, but are as those found in gods living in the Atma-sphere shaping se-ib-akhrn Shoot-ka-ba, the body's living beings.

Our great pyramids are now sealed, though we may project our Ka-Ba bodies by our thoughts, into these

chambers for making observations.

The stones are tested and the chambers are all sealed and are air tight. The vents were closed last night. They are building up great vacuum pressure now within their chambers. The stones and seals are tightened.

Spirit energies spiral motion and their powers are winding up.

The labs, far below the earth's surface at the base of the pyramids, are fully manned.

The elements fill the center crucible. They were all purified in that period of the solar-moon eclipse.

The sarcophagus is covered, and marked by the sounds of our sacred Se-Akh life-creating incantations, that were performed yester-night.

We have laid the great stones down upon their cover, to prevent the cover from flying off, with the release or change of vacuum pressures, when these, in the process of change, are being done.

The process is started then, and building up in the development of mass energy transmutation. We will be preparing sacred flying vessels from these, to be ready by the new moon.

I have heard the council will gather. There will be a determination of a great migration, and repopulation, as people will be moved across the vast sea at a future time.

They will settle in the land of Khem, following the path of the sun at the equinox to their destination, as the sun moves passing through the underworld.

We will follow it. We should be able to accomplish each migration by the passing days, following this with our new thought in flying vessels.

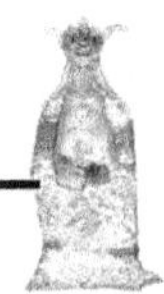

Others, fearing, move over land. They may take many moons to follow and that with great difficulty. But they will carry all possessions.

On wings of power, these gods are now, as we speak, inhabiting forces that are shared by their sacred spaces, to work miracles in their lattices.

Between their forces the mantras are created to give them intelligence, and talismans are made, to force their secret places, to conform to our thoughts, on their crystal planes.

They are powered by our Words of Power, being written now, and forced by the lifting of the coiled serpent, Le-Wau-Yah-Adon, in our meditations.

My world is enjoyed, even in this bliss of spirit, in the happiness discovered by being near them.

See . . . this staff flies by what I think.

I think . . . hmm! Strange memory, as are these feelings of senses once again and those faculties raise of Ma-Hi-Ma.

He begins, flexing his fingers and sensing the palms as felt by psychic powers, but falls deeper into somnambulistic forgetfulness, each time the hands open and close.

For a moment, he is a little confused by it, as he thinks. He relives his ancient life within the moments dream. He wonders now what was his yesterday, and the days before it, but drops the thought of it as suddenly.

Sage Time still directs this.

The object, by itself, begins to exhibit the weightless effect and that attracts his attention. It is a long rod with crystals breaking and accelerating light on each end, made of those completed substances born from their lab. It is covered by small lattices that

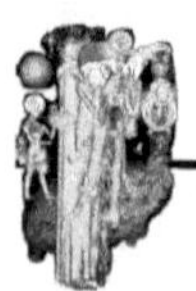

are variously colored all along geometries that are exposed and spaced evenly.

The rod suspends in space as easily as if uninhibited by any force of gravity. It is light but heavy, it is transparent but dense. It glows and releases a clouded mist and suddenly it hums a sound, that lulls them into forgetfulness and awakens them to the experience.

By the sound, it is suspended in the air, as if a god lifted it into the Atma-sphere by Mercury and imagination. It is there but not, since it appears and disappear, within the hum transforming its safe state, by the rhythm of its pulsation.

Solei

Her power is born. Our work has not been in vain, if we can produce enough of these to carry us away into the subtle Atma-sphere. By it we may not fall entirely into degeneration.

Some in our nation, cousins, sons and daughters, may be strong enough, and these by virtue may be allowed safe passage to immortality. Others may fall by the sheer weight of change.

Paris

Our crafts shall pass in clouds—drifting over the Earth like dreams on fleeting memories and we shall disappear into the sacred places.

Our thoughts will be lifted upon the Eagles back, and sent floating above our Kingdom of the Motherland in the perfect state.

And, like the Eagles eyes we shall gaze upon the Kingdom of the Motherland and challenge her mysteries, beyond the sightless glass of ignorance in the faultless

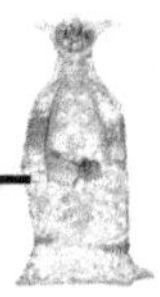

place.

These stones we have made from the gold stone of mystery. Sacred metals turned to glass and oil through fermentations in acid, and elevated to live by reincarnating in our urine, through those spirits living in our blood.

I shall see us move beyond the naught-naught gate under the cares of the Watchers who stand without.

Solei

Her forces shall bend before the power of the spoken thought, in the joy transmitted by her living testimony. The Mother may be delighted in this.

The Word of Delight shall be realized.

We shall pass beyond the systems of ignorance and mortal life.

We shall spy wearing ancient Rose in Red, bearing Cross of Gold, and realize our indebtedness to her treasury that we may deliver up our destiny, and our duty may be realized waiting on that Golden Age.

Solei suddenly changes in appearance staring around dark corners in the room, she has a feeling returning from what was forgot. Paris is indifferent and begins to speak.

Paris

What a vision this has come to be! All our . . .

My dear Solei, what troubles your thoughts?

Solei

Do you feel that?

Paris

*Appears the stars are on some tempered course . . .
perhaps . . . in the silence, I feel the restless firmament.*

Paris looks around concerned but more so, curious.

Solei

*More dear Paris, it brings pains to the center of my spirit
. . .*

The earth trembles.

Solei (Cont'd)

What was that? I have felt it again!

I fear.

What news of Sheea?

Paris

How's that?

Solei

*Is there any sign of Sheea? The time has passed overdue.
They've been away too long and I . . .*

Paris

*She and Caanon should be here soon. I have called them
back by my thoughts.*

Solei

*Such a long time away. I feel it taking us back to the
beginning.*

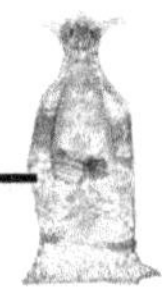

Paris

It is the sun living in the heart by the passion of loves ceremony. They are astride that Sun and are now as if traveling with it in the Universe. They live in that great fire by their solar life. So young, they dally in their love.

Solei

Lovely, I delight in hopes of their wellbeing.

Does this joy of theirs have a name that I may call it to me?

I am inspired by its solace, but I feel as if I am its neophyte, when it comes to removing the unwanted fears of imagination.

There is another tremor.

Solei (Cont'd)

I have felt it again!

Paris

A solace indeed. . . Recall the sacred place from whence you came and realize that the wilderness provides much counsel to awaken them into the hopes of their matrimony . . . The trials of youth.

What have you felt?

Solei

(Solei recovers her manners.)

Beloved Director, my mind at times is hazy by nature. When covered by the darkness of my own flesh. That distorts the Great Life in me by degrees.

But, I realize enough to know that you were young once.

Paris

Nearly . . . How shall youth be uncovered? By degrees? The ignorance of youth is unimaginable as we age. There lies the rude impressions on my mind and what is felt by the sphere of sensation.

So, let's bring delight in that generation of perfected love.

Who will be our guide? The great sun Shamesh by name and Math-Raem by design. That spirited by the seven voweled sign.

It is the light that comes and goes between the dark and light, between the subtle and the gross, by the grace of the subtle and the sacred ministers living in the same.

I have here taken up this Rod of Eltron, and by it evoked the letter "Heh" . . .

It is that Saint and aspirant representative of the breath of life, as if by the Hawk of Dawn, it has risen from the east, in the early hour breathing, sighing "Ham-Sa" into space from the beginning. By it all animals were raised and by it their spirits recognized. . . by their zodiacal signs . . .

Paris stops suddenly.

What have you been keeping here?

He goes to the chest.

Some hidden oracle of nature?

Solei

An oracle of the dreams found within our sacred Mysteries. It delights in the spirit of Immortal Man. It

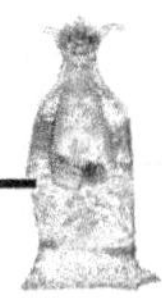

is the supreme principle of the universe, before delighting into the spherical lighted places that spread throughout the body of man.

The four poled powers have found their delights in the seven, and in this instrument lies the preparation that is felt in the union of our enlightenment.

Here I am inspired by the God of gods to awaken their ministering experience.

Paris

(Confused.)

A magical miracle? A dramatic, yet secret, profession?

Solei

(She laughs.)

From you? What secret Profession can be kept?

Paris

(He smiles, and peers over it, then stiffens standing straight.)

I love a mystery. I stand in the center of the balance on the crossed arms of strength equally effaced. Obliterated, I am in all four directions and into that above and below, and into that center space, but I feel as if I am by these nerves lock into it, fixed in place by the muscle strain.

I am also as if four-faced seeing equally in all directions. Turn me towards the east, my beloved Solei.

She turns him facing toward the east since he cannot move of his own grace. There is a pause . . .

It feels of blazing light here—some first form, like a

creature come upon nature's light. It touches my soul's sentiments.

I am standing between the pillars. This likened to the Temple but with power and great strength. These are the Great Pillars of power North and South behind the veil that awakens to a daylight before me in the east.

Solei

It brings with it the beginning of an entirely new era in our investigations. It is by the East drawing from the sun, and the central place from which the suns light comes.

It brightens up the darkened world in the morning of new life. There to face the cubical altar of the universe with its lamp and wand to guide us. This the lamp, and there by your side the Stones of Eltron. Together . . .

Paris

Ah! Some sacred preparation this . . . These clearly are directing powers pulling from all the eight dimensions, above-below, the North and South, the East and West, Within-Without by their eight infinities they break out the soul's destiny.

Solei opens the box to reveal a growing pyramid of light. He stands in awe as it expands and contracts.

Solei

Beloved Director, why stand between the pillars? The soul of Nature's here. Our temples shall say more in and through this conscious energy generation, than the winds that blow spirits through our valleys. We shall all be living by their wave of bliss.

Paris

Indeed. But, the wonder. I wear the robe of purity suspended in the light. It is the cloak of true religion.

Such an art. Such a preparation that enlivens our nerve centers. But I stand between the pillars of the North and South because this is the gateway to all subtle knowledge; profound in its occult spirit moving into grace, facing East I greet the sun and moon as they rise to meet the day and night.

Here and there placed, I am standing in the presence of the Reconciler before the light and darkness, and I unwind in the place where the circumambulation begins, as the Golden measure of our nature.

The light in me ascends in the spheres of life and light, as the heart in its center place expands to witness grace. The image of God is before me as if I am face to face with divinity.

To the west, I feel the darkness and the decrease of light, as if sent into the twilight. It is conceding.

Its sun is absent falling from the light.

It is the place where I proceed from the darkness into light. These angels are my waking space, and I stand inspired in their places as the record of time and grace.

Solei

These are the guardians and watchers. They appear by names surrounding the sun or the letter "Heh" assisted by the others. The instruments provide admittance, though this thing appears like those items similar in the sanctums in our household, here it is espied before us, the god between us, as an unimaginable beauty arising from

the Lord.

Paris

Yes, indeed, but it is different from the rest. Prepare the sensing of the elements and let us call up the ancestral generations.

I feel its power as Amon-Nu-Ra the subtle spirit field of unspun light. To the south the heat and dryness, to the North to dark and moist night, like those who attend to the Garments of the Mysteries they sit like shadows over me.

I follow the miracle of the sunlight.

Like a bursting heart, I sense its cup by the luster of its emanations, and as if a legend, it is born suddenly. I see it as if hanging and suspended in the lustral waters of creation, by the purification and consecration of love, and by the sacred light of vigilance.

It fills the room with wonder.

Our thoughts by it expand far into the ancient mist of spirit inspiring elemental gods of first beginnings, and their occult witness to formations.

Solei

Behold my beloved Director, the threshold of Time, the Temple of Light—the grandeur of our ancient heritage.

Lifting her hands —the pyramid lights up instantly within and becomes brilliant, the lights shift and other articles in the room begin to take on its light waving, as if powered by the glittered mass moving in the wind, shining outward from within.

Solei (Cont'd)

Behold the extension of my thought in time. There the Throne of Glory is sitting in the East with the fiery Hierophant to fill our world with Life and Light in the spirit of our wonder.

Power and light, Mercy . . . Wisdom, his voice is heard to recount the mysteries, by the vehicle of voice waking in my listening ear.

Speaking, I hear its voice to me saying, "Arise spirit from within, to the light, and to the commencement of our reason, to recognize the spirits mystery hidden in our joy, and the love of endless circumambulation."

Paris

What honor you bring into this House of Time. My soul is unleashed.

Before truth it is a vision! My eyes, like rain, fall in gentle streams of bliss, concealed by this heart now bursting, the ruptured by its nature as well, is now revealed. The soul, made naked by its wonder, is the bliss revealed as thunder and illumination.

Caanon and Sheea enter. They stand with arms held in archetypical Adam and Eve pose as they are blinded by this angel of light emanating in the room. Solei retreats into herself and throws a veil over the instrument. Paris breaks his spell and the thing is quickly silenced to nothing, and they move to cover it.

Sheea

Father!

Caanon

Our hearts are inscribed, as if rewritten by the wisdom of ancient texts in wonder.

The miracle of the Word has blinded us in this virtuous testament. We are revealed by its power. I felt lighted in the power of delight, and was lifted by its delicate animation.

We sensed the presence in this spirit, awakened by a primal thought of wonder. How is it possible?

The light is diminished and the box is closed. Solei and Paris greet Caanon and Sheea with the loving embraces of lost kin and their hearts burst in delight. Things are normal again.

Caanon (Cont'd)

Sorry for being away so long. We'd gone some distance before your call was felt. Our return was delayed. There is some strangeness among us.

Sheea

Some tense desire was awakened and it is witnessed by the signs seen in the reeds and rushes, and it is sung by the birds and screamed by the woodland animals.

We saw this in the wilderness beyond the southern wall. There we saw the outbursts of a strange consciousness, like a fire stirring in the earth . . . fire and smoke appeared from out of its inner world, and as it rose we were frightened by it.

Paris

Change is inevitable, as yet some reluctance to change

has been felt by our Kingdom of the Motherland. The strange desires now played on us, need not concern us at this time.

There are some days in which to discover its outcome yet, but I feel its tremor beneath us shaking the villages near the rivers. Its subtlety is indeterminable.

Sheea

The tides are shifting about the Mother-land. I have seen strange tides drawn out to sea and they returned rushing into shore destroying trees.

A strange force was with it and many of the trees were uprooted. Our stone villages stood shaking in the distance. One movement so remote as I have never felt before, and I as well have never felt such fear along the Kala-Hama-Ana.

Our sacred Kingdom of the Motherland—Her centers appear to drift moving in unknown magnitudes, beyond the limit of our senses judging this.

I am moved between the sun and it. I feel her unsteadiness and it trembles beneath my feet. The moonlight seems as madness. It lies beyond the sea and sky, and merges with the stars, as angels of divine intelligence transcribed within the Key of Time.

They are the first cause of this within the spirit of those millions of miles of preceding motion, masked within pitched scales with modal emphasis around their tonic root, as played by the massive instrument of God.

Paris

Cyclical shifts are the miracle of time. They are common with age, as vastly determined by their beginnings.

How old is the UNIVERSE, it is the oneness of this miracle. Such an instrument, a Life living as One Thing.

Caanon

Our youth is yet unstabled by the grounds beneath our feet! The soles of which are stirring even as we speak.

Our souls of youth, feel the shift too strongly, and drift with its transient pressure shift. I feel that gravity even now, and it disturbs the hairs that creep across the skin, standing there on end, these evoke those that stand up upon my head, and the spirit by which they mock me with the compressions they entreat. I am in their current liquified.

Paris

Youth is always plagued with instability and foolishness. I should not imagine.

Age has brought forth solidity in our wisdom. To form worlds and dimensions, Time becomes our chief and demiurge. To design and transform us, as befitting the Builder of the Temple, and thereby our character and maturity.

We are wrapped within its webbing, as if each turn was likened to the pearl grown amidst the salting sea. Knotted together these form the web of mystery.

Mother has her tremors. In nature, the inventor vast, is everywhere in anywhere, as the center appearing in everything, whose breathy spirit, as life, vibrates incessantly, where the creator is exposed, and by those powers they are revealed by his Word alone.

These are chanted into form as the instantaneous entity appears in everything. These tremors may be the

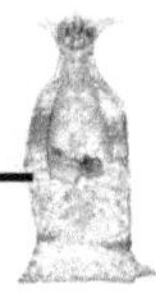

subjections of this spirit transforming into this.

Sheea

But there also lies our chief undoing, as the world Creator having willed it, and as sustainer having enjoyed it, but now as destroyer it has called for its return.

I fear our reluctance to our debts and consequence. This fear and debt has neither amassed a temple nor controlled a fire, but left us as shallow wells, emptied in our selfish youth, grasping the pathetic in our unsteadiness.

We can do nothing. Doing nothing we are too immature to recognize it, being so impatient in our ignorance.

Paris

Sweetheart, patience. Impatience cannot calm a storm.

Wait! We shall invoke the gods in due course to discuss this.

There are varying degrees of tension in earth, resolved when the tonic note within the constant chord or discord seeks the return, to resolve itself around the center of gravity. There the harmony or melody is created by the changes that are made in nature's contrasting keys.

These inspire tonal harmonics that are tuned to consciousness, frequencies, dynamics and qualities. But, lest we forget, spirit is a living entity. Time and change determine these in the hours of the day.

All creation follows that pattern of universality in resonance for that driving force. It is keyed in the first cause. This is for the dynamics, and this drawn toward a specific frequency in wave-force periodicity.

That property stores or builds up pending its release.

There is as easily the small transfer of energies of superconsciousness, as load bearing specific qualities stress between varying storage systems in nature.

These may be agreeing thru attunement or they may disagree contrasting by that grave will that is dysfunctional by the awkwardness of its design.

These models resolve first within electron or finite densities, as would be all resolvability found in the most minute subatomic wave form density that tie patterns smaller than a molecule.

Each of these form individually as finite gravity wavefields that contribute to the whole, and as a whole they unite as one within their centers.

If we change our center, we may change their center state.

These fields are properties are all pulled from the center in and out. That center is God whether finite or united as a whole or One Thing curved in space, and that power is the power of our return to zero, transformed into the miracle of time.

These contributes to its quality of agreement or disagreement by the very nature of their repetition and by that intelligence in design repeated by the Word or voiced spirit and its breath.

That, as well, by the powers of life and its ability to divide and multiply on the Tree of Life, and by these unfolding intelligence.

These universal lives are driven by the sun from pole to pole, North and South, and they spin by the power of the sunrise, and change the season as they spin around the sun, as they gyrate under those fields inspired by the stars.

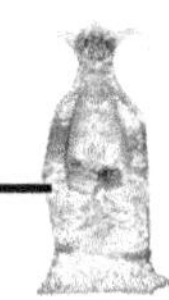

These solar powers shape the patterns for macro and microscopic magnetic fields of intelligence that rule our lives. These determine natures currents through spirit, fire, water, earth and air. The wind and rain clouds grow and follow these magnetic field. They determine the weather for the growing seasons.

The modal fields are those properties created and impregnated with life, and they are energies of superconsciousness, embodied by that sperm of generation, first inspired in the living nucleus by the Breath of God from the beginning.

We cannot alter any of this. Therefore it is the Will of God.

We have not determined this. It is by the Will of God as determined by these states of superconsciousness.

What is born of miracle can only be refined by it. Nature follows only the Will of God and cannot redefine it or chaos that is boundless would ensue.

We are inspired and our lives are determined by it, save by grace and love as a consideration, but we are serving at its finite table, born of the Sun, Moon, the stars and by these we gather at the breath of life and the spirit of the earth Mother. She who is beyond this matter and composting life and graveyard of the elements.

What is this unrest with you all? I am forever silent and at peace. Be at peace with me in this. We are not the bodies. We are not the mind.

Therefore, discord or concord never follow us. They are resolved in that root eternity, unmoved within our centers.

It is peace and silence that surrounds me thoughtless

Sheea

Father, upon the currents of our Kingdom of the Motherland is felt a . . .

That thought becomes suddenly super-sensual and all are drafted into a furtive energy, as if all are brought into the power of a sudden storm.

Obscured scenes appear and amplified by sounds that begin to echo in the atmosphere.

The sound produces tension in the muscles and nerve endings, as there is first a fire that is electrified within them, and as suddenly they are hit within, by the airy icing sense, with nerves stirring in a chill.

Hairs excite and stand on end, and their breath oscillates between hot and cold, as if within them they are lit by the dire winds of the firmament.

Thoughts become lightly audible as they lose self-control, and by their pressures these thoughts turn outward into sweat, and their energies collapse to near exhaustion.

There are voices heard, or are attempting to be heard, as if sounds were coming from the future. They are rattling the moments that they are communicating in. Faintly they are recognized.

In the air are seen scrying images in their super-state, in the moment there is an hour in the instant, in that period of contemplation, as they have been hit by its sudden timeless wind.

These miracles fly by with their sounds listing, as they are revealing phrases from scenes that appear in their imagination, and their senses are awakened by the future dialog, and there are tensions. The uncommon avatar is felt with his approaching.

These tensions are echoed by the Downward Seeing Lord, who appears as if he is the One. Complete before the fall.

They are as suddenly shaken to their senses as the sounds are withdrawn and these slowly fade away in silence. All are relieved. It seemed to be a lifetime lived within an instant. There is a moment of silence before Solei speaks.

Solei

The beloved!

Khan Gu approaches. He comes from the valley of the winds.

Paris

His presence is felt. Unmistakable . . . I have not heard it like this, with such clear access to those dimensions beyond the world, stayed by those forces that surround him. He approaches deep in contemplation and that thought is overwhelming.

Sheea

He reveals himself . . . by his thoughts in me, I sensed the cause of our delay!

Caanon

We passed along Kala-hama-ana on the currents of Zazil. Lightning in the atmosphere seemed to crisscross

our path, cutting into the landscape as if following with us. There, along the ridge, as we passed along that mountaintop, all appeared still, while the world spun around us on its axis. The air was spinning violently, but nothing moved. The world was untouched by it.

We became immersed in the thought; envisioned in the moment, running quickly below the Temple of our Forest Cover. Even there, beneath their limbs hiding from the fierce encounter, we could not escape and so encountered it.

There the Tree of life suddenly swayed unimaginable to the first cause beginning—in the Breath of Light passing with the wind. We felt the power of its instability.

We could see those forces moving heavily in the flow through the atmosphere between the spheres of energy—as above-so below.

The atmosphere was as suddenly fading, and we can only describe that feeling to our senses over time, but these were active layers, still relevant within us, and these sounded as the warning that hounded us like jackals through the wilderness.

These warnings were as if, suddenly they were forces awakened by invisible creatures that were predatory, sensing meat before their table, and we, our lives, seemed to be their staple.

We prayed to Atma-sphere and called upon the Gu, and their forms subsided into the spirit of subtle atmosphere, vanishing into air.

Solei

What new rites are performed by the member nations or other city states?

Sheea

The Temple of the Khan is being charged with the emergence of the Twelve members of the solar council that he's called before it. From the planets they are drawn to meet our members at the table.

Paris

No? What? All Twelve?

The seven seen and those unseen?

Caanon

Oh, they are seen now. Representatives of the council have gathered there to consult with the oracle. They are joining from all the united nation states.

Representatives, I feel, of our ominous estate as well, too near a conflagration. They have called for emergency relief. All the city states were as concerned everywhere we went. But it is undecided.

Sheea

Oblations then, to the Holy One ensue.

Solei

Something is in the . . .

Khan Gu in his magnificence approaches through the doorway. His presence unfolds energies that flash across the room, from out of empty atmosphere, as if a sudden spark is lit. Space is overwhelming and they can hardly stand.

The Khan Gu appears as if out of atmosphere. He emerges as something subtle to become a condensate descending into energy

with a bright flash of electric light. Thoughts have preceded his entry, and they reveal the nature of his presence, by the letters in the living record.

This name is echoed in the mind as the father of light. Two voices speaking together are heard, as these letters named A-BA-BA Aba, suddenly appear, and they come revealing the powers of the Father *A-Bet* as they are speaking from beyond reason simultaneously by the words that are timeless as they are overlapping in the mind.

A

I am come . . . Discuss we will . . . reveal.

B

I am come . . . I am come . . . We have been . . . Long .

A

Blessed . . . We have been . . .

B

Blessed Be the land of Mu! I am in its sweetness the wake of sacred letters filled with love and wonder.

A

Blessed be the land! Blessed thrice great Khan Guru! Ignite as light before him. Blessed be the land!

Khan Gu

Peace, I am come among you, to prepare within our time, a remnant of our sacred heritage for future generations. Blessed be the Light, the spirit of the ineffable. Blessed be the Land!

Blessed be the land of Mu! Sacred and honorable, Mu! Blessed be the land!

Mu the sacred! Mu the Blessed. Treasured in the rounds of Spirit Energies. Spirit immortality orbiting in the Garland Earth; surrounding the inspired, mirroring the miracle of Time!

Mimic mirror, mimic cosmic character, lighted by the gods, on the Tree of Life.

Our heritage signifies the benevolence of generations that have performed her rituals honorably!

Sit down! Deflate thy self-image. Humble thyself now! I stand before you to represent the honor of our Kingdom of the Motherland!

He raises his hand at right angles by his arms, with all five fingers upright and exposed. All cross arms slammed to the chest in Salutation, while dropping to one knee, except Paris who salutes smashing his chest with the right arm over heart, a left arm in the air forming the right triangle (345), and his legs crossed by the feet, responding the spinning representative of these, with the open hand five fingered sign of the elements that are ominous.

The fingers are very long as if they'd been stretched from childhood. In the center of his palm is revealed the image of the sacred eye that is championed by the heart. Painted and powerful it is as if appearing that it is the Endless Seeing Eye.

Khan Gu (Cont'd)

We are welcomed by our devotion to her chivalry and the revelations born of character. They bring the gods to bear down witnessed by their lights upon us, and smile with goodness and good health, by the igniting of the starlight, and their patterns, reflecting in the flesh of night! We stand together as one witness, come before, to

gather here in the spirit of the moonlight.

There, above our temples, the heavens, by witnessing our signs, ignore us. These who bring us good fortune, have become the flouting now.

We have prayed, and our prayers once answered have now ignored us, they are fated by the inevitable that even the gods cannot betray.

Their bright eyes enflame the night of the matter forming spirit. We have seen the new bright stars expanding that appear out of daylight, with bright surrounding light.

Their patterns cannot deny us they have aggravated Time. Our fortunes lie inside our provocated whims, but these appear by the heavens as the ominous signs of God's ignoring energies, as stars exploding and expanding out of sight. Their stars once counted have disappeared from night.

What can be gained by the death of these gods, who have sacrifice themselves? The shock waves will soon come down upon us from their light, like the thunder in the distance.

Our fate and fortunes are before us. We are the prisoners, passing as shadows witnessed by the properties of Time.

Therefore, awakened to our destiny, by its power I have come tonight. We are shaken by design, as seen in the stars within the night.

Paris

ARAMA Atitich, Khan Gu!

Central fire is cooled when submerged in water, your person and powers are superior to all things, Sovereign,

Lord. Immaculately conceived!

They all together then genuflect on one knee bowing, even Paris, falling to the ground, before arising simultaneously, as if in military form. Rising side by side.

Sheea

We were awaiting your arrival.

He stares long, with blackened eyes compassionate and filled with deep concern, upon the crowd. The long Sandy brown hair rolls in ringlets to his shoulders.

Khan Gu

Have these intimations also revealed the nature of the coming?

Caanon

Your arrival has been our primary concern, but we have heard . . .

Paris

We have been reflecting upon matters relating to the sudden emergence of the Twelve members of your council, who have left their stars to appear before you now.

Khan Gu walks around silently. Deliberate movements and gestures like these cannot be described as even imaginable, weighing deep every word to come. He tries not to dominate, but does so nevertheless. His sheer pure presence and appearance makes our words inaudible. He attempts to calm them, who stand stiff and motionless, by his suggestions for their peace.

Khan Gu

The Earth is calm. Winds blow down the Valley and whistle through the boughs. We've even insinuations of a beautiful night . . . There!

He points to the East and the emergence of the first signs of the moon.

Khan Gu (Cont'd)

The moon will rise into fullness tonight.

Pausing his mood shifts.

Khan Gu (Cont'd)

Do you love this land?

He speaks as he is turning and facing Paris who is the strongest among them, and the one that is never stirred that is suddenly shocked by his appearance.]

Paris

What melancholy.

Khan Gu

We are old Paris. Perhaps too old.

On my walk here, the early hours were at first very dark and sullen. Surly, the moon disappeared and turned into sunlight, soft as the dew, it came down resting upon the fields.

It wet the grains; swayed on the stalks that set against the Sun all through the day, reflecting like a flame amidst a golden flickering, and instead of illuminating the surroundings, it cast an ominous shadow on the green,

where otherwise pure sunlight would have been. That atmosphere was ominous and felt as if the world were watching me.

I have felt somehow relieved, that were it not for the glory of the Kingdom of the Motherland, these strange times and signs would be my undoing, even as I witnessed this.

Paris

My dear old friend.

Paris moves to the Khan—but the Khan Gu holds up his hand to stop him.

Khan Gu

When our people were conceived out of the myth, out of ancient mysteries preordained, our mold was formed out of reverence, duty and devotion. . . and that, for the righteous elements upon us—elements under the guise of a hidden Light—suspended upon the Breath, in darkness, by the sacred mystery.

There was a fondness and delight spirited by the emergence of daylight.

Thus became the Breath, that sacred element, in its first form.

All that is, exists out of the Breath, in the mouth of time. Our cosmic fields follow this by its whispers that fly with us, into our conception like the mercurial wind.

It breathes the elements . . . in and out . . . in one naked breath of life.

I asked the Gods of the spoken Breath . . . yes . . . from what strange proximity of the world do we come?

Hmm, hmm! (laughing to himself).

"Ah, Hah!" they replied, "From the strangest portions of the yet unknown," and they then pummeled me with breath, and I nearly went unconscious by it.

The currents of our lands are restless. The cycles are shifting, and my thoughts scatter into heavy laden muse.

Solei

We have felt them Beloved Gu.

Caanon

There's something troubles you.

Khan Gu

I have felt, within the depths of my thought, the mystery in dreams and meditation.

In a vision, I have witnessed many unknown meanings, wherewith the future is disbanded.

In a dream, I beheld a whirling sound that lifted my thoughts into a dark place, and there in some spaceless mode of silent witnessing, I realized the spirit of Nothing that did exist to me, as if everything were flying in emptiness, as the Awareness merging into the unconceived Eternity, and I became the edge surrounding everything conceived within creation, by the illustrious Seeing Eye, even that place beyond the stars left behind, which suddenly became as a speck of nothing to me.

Then, of a sudden, out of the eastern horizon of eternity I beheld a lovely lady; plummeting through

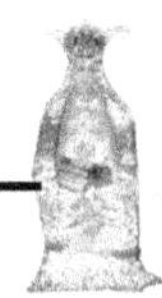

the darkness, leaving streams of trailing fires where she passed. She was in tears and she felt to me, as being the daughter of Fire and Wind and Rain.

She bore from her bosom the fruits of the Kingdom of the Motherland, and taking these in hand; transformed them into vaporous clouds of heated mass, which suddenly dispersed in sublimation.

There, a tablet of fire, water, air and earth spoke, as if from that spirit in her center that she had risen from.

There a Massive obelisk suddenly appeared and next to her it was all cover o'er in letters.

She, the more than Beautiful, spoke in vibrant streams of chanting letters, and there they appeared in squares of patterns that formed, as on a platformed tableau where they crossed, vibrating in their centers as the squares of magic letters that are thought.

And when the fire cooled, their nurture of spirit energies like angels fell in condensations upon all the darkened world, as the fields of matter were, before their natures are transformed.

Paris

How is it meant to be?

Khan Gu

Beloved Paris, your work has gained a great delight, a benefit clearly upon our community, and upon the people of our Motherland. But I fear the time has come, like me, for you too, so near to death to realize our shortcomings.

The time is come for our beloved progeny, to proceed to travel out among the peoples of the world, and

communicate our learning. They among the others shall descend in the fall of Time to become as matter born. We have spoken of this before and have not looked forward to the day. They shall be a shadow to us and we as well to they. . .

Paris

Yes, but my honored Gu, there is great need for our service here. There below, is the dead and dying world.

They may be called to the world of Beauty.

It is assured. . . What voice speaks to the beauty and fairness to our piety? The Great, Great, Great, Thrice Great in the three worlds, in honor of the Mind of the Great Lord has said,

"O' you people born of earth, given over to drunkenness and sleep—stopped in ignorance of God. Cease! Be sober and abandon your excess. As inheritors through generation after generation of this dying world, now be called back to truth in living light.

Do not be lured into the world of brutes, who seek death and slothfulness with such dullness and debauchery.

Wherefore, as Fools, why be made unreasonable with sleep. Why be delivered as such by the Hanged Man unto death, when you have the power to partake of immortality by the wisdom of the breath.

Turn the mind. Long have you dwelt in darkness. Abandon the death of night!

Seek the Day of Glory's light! Change the mind.

Put away the darkness of that dark night, where that shaded light of ignorance is filtered by the shadows, delighting in arrogance and ignorance.

Intelligence is wiped away, where Wisdom has no sacred place.

We may then look with favor with those who are faithful, and heed the warning, and take sworn testament of those who would be raised.

We shall say, rather than by that ignorance take delight, and partake in the fruits, and feast on immortality.

Turn away from the power inherited with regeneration—continuously partaking of this death by returning again and again into this world of constant incarnations—returning back into this realm of compost and corruption—fumbling blindly, like the dumb, trampling in the dark in search of Truth."

I mean to say . . .

It may well be that our fruits should be inspired into all the races that are beyond our reaches, above and below us, before our decomposition. Yet if there is . . .

Khan Gu holds his hands up to stop Paris.

Khan Gu

Oh, your thought precedes your words. Great accomplishments need not be laid aside ... No, not yet. They are bound by a threefold bond of mortality by their earthly incarnation.

It is a narrow place and they are in that wandering as the soul in darkness, having forgotten the world of beauty that their eyes once looked upon, by that blindness of mortality.

Two contending forces are constantly served to unite against them, in the battles of the day, where these converge as three, in forming the spirit world of senses,

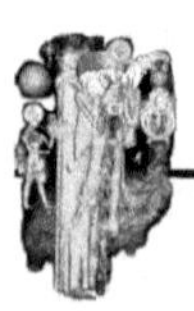

and their lock with finite elements to initiate them.

We pray for them that they may be guided by a light rushing forth from them in a single ray, as a pillar to stand between the forces of Good and Evil excess.

Paris

But, yet you are asking us to leave, and spread ourselves far from our sacred shores, to merge with these animals. Beyond the safety of our Kingdom of the Motherland, that lies far above the Kingdom of Mal-kat, before even that Garden of Paradise.

If they would seek the light, they must be obligated. Nothing comes of those who bear no responsibility. That is the mark of cowardice for those who profane what are sacred things. Are they ready to take this obligation?

Khan Gu

Perhaps.

I am asking for what is asked of me. To give them a straight pathway through the hidden knowledge, unlike the path of nature, continuously confused by undulations, and the windings turning here and there on the path the Serpent's taken.

Where is the straight and narrow way between them?

I am asked to help the races increase in virtue so that, even now, I am placed between them. Far below us on this mighty Tree, they are seen to aspire to our virtue, or to our censure.

They may come through me. I may initiate them by their aspiration to remember this day as a marked one in existence, for those who cultivate the mental attitude

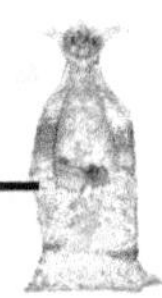

worthy of our order, with honor and due reverence for the Lord of Luminescence.

But for what reason? The whole is greater than its parts. They may in the Presence of the Lord of the Universe become humbled before the Great Light of the Mysteries, and we may together partake as sparks of that Great and Unsupportive Life and Light.

It may be that this wisdom touches on their consciousness. That borders on the Garment of Flames that sweep the boundaries of this Universe.

It is the season. They may study well. Some may leave. Others not. Not so lucky, we, either way. We may laugh at them, but that would be a tragedy.

We may only win the world when we win the peace. Silence is its remedy.

The unimaginable lies before us . . . and all that Time forgot stands to win our favor. They may in the presence of the Lord of the Cosmic Entity, pledge of their own free will to be sworn, to keep secrets of these miracles, from the unworthy, violent and ignoble persons, and to be counselled in our laws, rules and policies, that they may learn to keep good company.

It may profit us to advance others less favored in this pursuit. They may be pledge to not burden us in their personal desires, for personal aggrandizement, or to use these powers to harm another knowing well the consequence.

Our lives demand detachment. That is inevitable. This precludes that period to follow with us, to draw us into the iron age, which has begun.

Death, disease, destruction. . . these watchwords follow

with the tide in the great force to level the world, for provoking one's evil ways.

Time has turned to unveil lost kingdoms. The age of vice. We may be there when they are called back again.

Now, the demoness comes and with her the fangs, the age of strife and discord, lies and deceit, and with these creatures they invoke the wretched self. They are wholly answerable for their moral and ethical crimes.

Naked, the lips will be unimaginable witness to false tongues, and they will stand by those with the gnashing teeth, and of those to come before the Scale of Truth, for answering against the life in the age of Judgement, at the door of death.

We will stand by with these and be witness to it, to determine if they pass or return to live again.

Spirits will degenerate. It will be inevitable. Morality will fade with the young. Rulers will be unreasoned with. Taxes will be over whelming and unfair.

Sworn to duty, these may be committed to be bred with reason and thereby commit to memory the laws, rules and principles, whereby the Creator may do great works through these. It is that age of vice and disagreement.

Duty performing as one's human service will disappear, and their unfair tax collections and practices will appear as divine gifts to many, for all purses crave so as to fill academics with the greed of self-indulgences, deemed justifiable by reason of the moral insanity.

Worse. All talk of God will disappear in the dark and dirty age, as man becomes the demon of these false sympathies, and devotion will devolve into the ignorance desired of academies filled with false arguments, and the

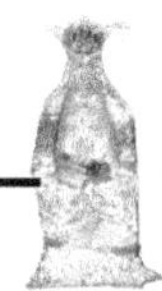

bloodied creatures lust, will be consumed by sexuality and wars.

There will be no men of honor. No women of charity or chastity will be gathering on the stage of honor and dignity.

Righteousness will be displaced by intolerance and ignorance of the truth and sympathy will fade with the lack of sensitivity to the Divine Instrument, and worse, all children will grow in their societies like zombies listing in the night. Their will, subjected to the false suggestions of false teachers and their lies.

They will be the nothing-knowers, full of vice pretending to be wise, while filling their bellies with intoxicants that lead them, in their stupor, to the cliff of death to die at night, all alone in dying places with their loved ones standing by. These will grow darker in every generation.

We will leave our peace and safety here, to serve and give the gift of hope in hopeless places.

Paris

But the races could journey here where they may be safe. Rather than follow by that shadow of death, if no other way than this. Here they may promise to uphold integrity and forever endeavor to persevere, in the pursuit of perfect knowledge and the Wisdom of the Father, by his graces.

Solei

Beloved Gu, many great works are being handled now, and even the finest nearing their fully created form. I dare not desecrate what may be sacred in their eyes, but they may not keep the seal of secrecy.

They may not find joy in our Arcanum. They may stand beside unbalance Severity with cruelty. They may stand by unbalanced Mercy to permit evils to exist unchecked.

We may only stand watch as guardians of the Threshold. They may become undaunted by the difficulty in study, unchecked by perseverance; avoiding those actions requiring purification and preparation. Our peace may be unsettled here.

Sheea

I fear the Khan speaks truthfully. In our vision along the Kala-hama-ana, our mind was filled with scenes on high, beyond the reach of Glory, Wisdom and Understanding.

We stood and gazed from Nul-kin-tan, the center lighted by the Sun, on the mountain top, and there Caanan and I peered out in reflection upon a lost and forgotten art that covered our civilization; and there a sadness fell upon the face of the whole of creation . . . it was there before our eyes.

Paris

You are the mighty Khan. Time has sanctified these blessings handed down by your designs, but the desire now appears greatly misunderstood.

Perhaps only our influence becomes more profound, upon the course, with regard to the Races.

There, from the safety of our place, our morality and virtue may shine upon the nations and we may protect their lives by sending saints to greet them in the mean.

Their darkness may become the harbinger of light. These creatures are as creatures bred in the abyss of

darkness. From that darkness, they came to be born as the witness to the world of experience, born from that primeval sleep.

That soul follows them again and again saying unto them along the way, "I am that spirit that formulates in darkness. Child of Earth, the light shines within the darkness, but the darkness comprehends nothing."

But those unpurified and unconsecrated they cannot pass, save by the path of the elements, and along the way by the revelation of the Names, of those watchers and those guardians.

That is the path of initiation upon which course the races . . .

Khan Gu

The course of the races is not the chief concern, but the needs and desires of the People of the Kingdom of the Motherland are mine. They scatter to the East, South, West and North by way of their elements.

My first love rests upon our community. Not every star has given lives the blessing of seeing life witnessed by descending and condensing into form, but our star has made this the subject and the promise as a blessing, and we are subjected to this in the Kingdom of the Motherland.

We may consecrate these as they move passing by Fire, Water, Earth and Air.

The races fend for their nature, their days of drudgery and condensation are numbered into infinity, but to what aims our people's chief requirements tend, this is my prime estate. Whenever the Sun . . .

Khan Gu passes by the box holding the Lighted Pyramid. Suddenly even his hairs stand on end.

Khan Gu (Cont'd)

What power is here?

He turns and stares at Paris, and with a sense of urgency repeats more forcefully. This time not asking but commanding.

Khan Gu (Cont'd)

What power is here! The East? The Light appearing as it happens I feel the Golden Day.

Paris

Solei's dream. Meh-Ra, Mathray-Em the spirit of the Voice conceived first in the dream before the power of Time and dimmed light of Man.

Solei

The power of the first Light; generating in the first form, the Word of God unmasked in form as the pure instrument of dreams.

She opens the box slowly.

Solei (Cont'd)

Lord, to my soul's amazement, it tends to my desires.

She concentrates and the room increases in her Light.

Khan Gu says nothing. All stand aside as Khan Gu approaches. All watch with fear as his power alone is sheer desperation, and so, fearing not to speak for desecration, but for what could be generated here.

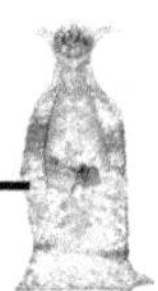

He stretches out his hands. He appears to concentrate, at first thoughtful, but it grows, and the power that streams off him into the room fulfills itself, by shaking waves of moving forces that are vast and roll through the edifice, and into the members standing there, who are half in fright and half in delight.

It becomes magnificent, to a brightness beyond the capabilities of sight, it is so blinding in the light that it moves them all near to unconsciousness.

A terrific humming commences becoming louder and louder, and then voices are heard, almost as if there were thunder in the voices rolling through the room by the sound.

Its voice is transformed into strangeness, timeless . . . music, names and cultures were heard, all roll from the past to future times, along with revelations—visions of the future appear to crawl out of their dark destruction, like specters in the night.

There is an exploding sound that is deafening, as if the world were blown apart, and total darkness is dropped and the sound of Khan Gu's voice is heard speaking in the atmosphere that is orating out of mind, his tongue is silenced and memories appear in the Atma-sphere with visions of the future time.

The Khans eyes are fixated with a stare that focuses on the instrument, and the meaning and the wonder sounded, as if the voice in the atmosphere became starry ghosts appearing from the Atma-sphere.

> *EN-HA-RA- Shin-Ma -Kalac.*

> *Unbalanced force is malicious driving creation to destruction. Unbalance Mercy but feebleness unable to stand for what is good. File down the Tree of Life.*

> *Unbalance Severity is but subjugation creating without purpose and a theater of consequence. The Will of God is righteousness. Come in the light of Wisdom and*

Understanding.

Come in the Mercy of the light. The light has healing treatments for the cure and comforting of genius unfolding in its timed partitions of illuminating acumen.

Come in the power of the light. Become inspired in the Beauty of its genius. Come light inspired illumination of our genius.

It is done! I am the Breath of the Soul—the Fire in Earth—the Cosmic World inspired, Sam-e-kha in the Cosmic Stars the Nayana, the sacred eye, I am moving thus, Na-Nara-Ayana! The spirit on the waters.

I am the miracle insight living on the inside. I am Universal. The Soul flying suspended, I am in the darkness.

I am the depth and breadth of space that is absolute. I am now beyond the stars. Even they cannot contain me but are as a single twinkling in my eye, as they are left flashing in the shadow far behind.

Holy is God, Holy the Father, the delight of all things imaginable. I pass into that pure Atma-sphere beyond the endless edge as passing the spirit and the stars.

Holy is God for I am in that beginning ONE, whose will is absolute, and his rule by mystery of that WORD is realize in the spirit of the powerful form.

I Am the star beyond and before the form, and they, mere twinkling's in the night that pay homage to this containment of "I Am I."

Those miracles made as playthings, by these forces drawing them to us in daylight. Thy are mere shadows performing miracles by their gradients, by their

shadowing in their light.

Holy is God, Omniscient-Ancient. Holy that determined omnipresent ONE that is self-known, creator omnipotent, and omniscient in the knowing.

Holy that Life that is known, in knowing as the Knowing-Form of omniscience.

By all this that is his delight in Knowing-All that is his to be known alone. All this known the God is manifest in those spirits who are known.

Only the God who knows has showed the sightless to know them by him, when made aware of His knowing them.

Without the knowing, they are unknown.

By all these I AM pure attributes. I Am the saved as the saving entity, within these faculties that make the knowing known.

They are in him. His own. They by Him are known alone—Pure Awareness and Identity.

Where that place of fear is unknown, by that bliss of illustrious courage, I Am, in the Fearless and the Measureless.

Holy Lord; You are that Word alone, and by that Word all things appear and vanish, and are established by their knowing form.

For the invisible things suddenly appearing, you are the cause before the forms, and in creation, even those miracles that are above and below, the midnight and midday.

The worlds, they are the unseen, and in this power they are clearly seen.

I Am, as understood, by the Being, I Am that created Lord. Made One, in his eternal power I Am that immortal confidence, by that monarchy as Godhead supported by the form.

Holy Lord of the Universe. Lord of whom Nature is that image of illumination. Lord that shines in me, born from the sperm-seed of Righteousness as the image in the form.

First form of God Alone, I Am in that One Union yoked to divinity.

I Am, in all oneness conceived by that image appearing on the staff of life.

I Am given life alone by the sperm of animation as the fire of spirit appearing as that universal life.

Holy, You Are alchemical destiny. Holy Lord of the Universe of formless miracle-making, omnipotent, alive, beyond all powers that are born, beyond what can to be known, arising out of that nothing, and rising to become the most-minute and endless merging, into the grandest form.

No limit can be extended beyond the limit of that miracle of design. No creator is known or unknown save the One alone, whose spirit the spirits even live by, and manifest by that sacred Eye, as seeing entities.

Seeing from the center they are lighted by that sight.

Holy You Are. Lord of the Universe, whose presence is unknown, hidden by the omniscient and omnipresent unlimited.

Holy in that excellent Sanctum by design that has no restriction in the perfection beyond incomprehensible unconceived imagination.

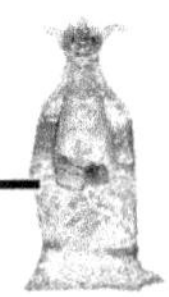

Holy Lord, beyond the praises of these words of mine. What can be praised by those living by the days, who cannot fathom their own graveyard.

Save by your presence we are awakened and awakened by lifetimes made, and remade, in that One before all things are formed.

I Am, raised beyond the spirit of the sacrifice, rarer than that artifice of the vast Wordless enterprise.

I am offered as the pure soul in the sacrifice. With this heart driven through, by the sting of love and devotion. I Am Light.

Here I am the slain animal man of many dimensions, collapsing in your battlefield of light, but my heart is one, take it with my love and devotion, blessed spirit of this night.

You are praised by my wordless silence. You are the unutterable, as I am before you the unforgivable, as humbled as you are generous in my sight.

May I be forever without blemish. May I walk the everlasting path of righteousness forever in that sight.

May I know all what must be known. By your mercy look mercifully on me.

Here is my prayer:

That they all may be one; as you are ONE, Father ABBA, as you are One in me, and as I Am One in you, that they also may be one in us, and the world may witness this, by their words, even as You are witnessing this in me.

And by the glory which You have given me, I give them back to You; that they, being one with me, they may be One, even as we are One.

For I am in them, and you are in me, and we may be made perfect in that Oneness. And the Kingdom of the Motherland may know who has sent me forward to give this message to them. For I have loved them, as You now have loved me. And, I am that Beloved.

These here are my everlasting brothers, sisters, friends and cousin born from the elements of our Kingdom of the Motherland.

By that grace witness this of me for I have been blessed to fuel the lives of the blessed, and so, to offer these of mine to thee, let this One spirit be my destiny.

ABBA, I will, by the power of my will, so that those who live with me in the Kingdom of the Motherland, will be with me where I am; that they may behold my glory in You, which You have given me: for Your loving me, has loved me here, in this place before the foundation of the world. By this our destiny is fulfilled.

We are in ignorance and I beg not to be ignored in consequence for our suffering, for this has paid the wages, for the abuses we have witnessed, and for those lesson that have plagued us, over and over again.

Lives that are repeatedly being lifted to celebrate honorably the dishonored course of our abusive generations.

Enlighten these and us with grace. I believe. I bear witness to this, and I will forever cherish this in that embrace, within our breasts, and I will make my way in Life and Light, and spill over in the confidence of your Eternal Loving Bliss.

I am that lighted Yod-Jyoti flame.

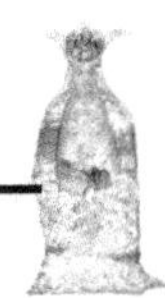

Blessed! Blessed! Blessed! Thrice blessed, Be, the Father of the Kingdom of the Motherland.

Beautiful as that immortal day of Man. That Man would be sanctified as you have given to him Life and light and all the power of this delight to spread love across the Kingdom of the Motherland.

Bear this record to the future, for I shall be their living memory.

For I am their Khan ḏḥwty!

I am their beloved Sai-Amon!

I am their Shivasai-Tehuti!

I am that power born Khanḏḥwty! The King of Life and Light, Kuth-Umi.

Chapter Three

Peace ensues. Sounds become subtle, relaxed and quiet. Energies slowly move up and down, spinning in a wheel exciting the Tree of Life vitalities. The gods stir.

Though the sound cast is a faint whisper, it is airy. We can hear it. The imagination flies to and from the root cause of reality, anticipating the next transition, as the cloud of energy is spinning in the generation of light.

Breathy and faint, the light follows the breath, as in the Word that is spoken. It is Lighted breath. It is a spherical galaxy of soft wind made of Atma-sphere forming spirit.

It is tuned to that region of space beyond the atmosphere. Clear-space opens to the entity alive in the cloud, and it is turned in the field of Cosmic Consciousness. This spinning theater of energy evokes the subtle mystery, spinning clockwise-anticlockwise simultaneously in a field that is shaped as a galaxy.

There, in this miracle, the stars live shining by the gods. Space-formed creatures these. Alchemical sources fulfilling human destiny.

There, in the lighted breath, slowly an angel appears. It breaks through the subtle matter of our vision. First to supply us with a simple luminous blue-green form. Slowly becoming dense, it materializes shapes to reveal the appearance of our Sage, appearing as before.

His power is drawing breath energy from the atmosphere and storing it. Power is spinning in a cloud formed by that breathing spirit, condensing and contracting, thicker and thicker.

Breathing deep and heavy, Sage Time is surrounded by the thicker energy, formed of that life-spirit of super-conscious Mystery, in

the materialized particles, of the essence of immortal life.

The light of creation seen in it, blinds us by our nearness. But there is love and bliss felt, to satisfy us, radiating from it.

We feel the transitions of heat and cold. It shifts to break within the prison of the shell it forms, and that slowly settles, as the blue-green atmosphere expands, glowing in a light magenta of life force.

Still heard from the beginning the background drums are heard once again beating time. This is the nature of time from the beginning (*Bereshith*).

Sage Time

The ancient fires raged in Darkness . . . time tolled out her magic 'neath the canopy of spirit shining stars, from inside galaxies it delighted in the miracles provided by first forms.

Sage Time begins to slowly circle orbiting, and turning like a sphere, light footed, before us, emulating the planets passing by a sun.

He walks, his footsteps moving 'round a finite region, as a planet in its orbit.

He evokes spirit from his person, invoking fire in the surrounding as a light, appearing out of air and water elements.

Each step by its angle is stepped, and marked appropriate in its rhythm, to the meaning of the time.
By direction the movements seen are calculated to mark the passage of time, and the movement of ideal attributes.

He inspires the ground he walks upon, and that dust becomes alive. It is ignited by the mind in evocation, shaping markings drawn with dedication. Then a light mist as fog surrounds him.

He calls the subtle spirits down with magical incantations to enter into their forms.

Then he stops heavy breathing and turns softly begins speaking:

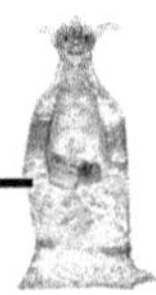

Sage Time (Cont'd)

Dust and Ash! Flame and Fiery invocation! Here form amidst us, one and All!

Water - Breath of strange and powerful illumination! One form, come before our summoned call!

He strikes the earth with his staff and steps deep footed into the earth. The earth buckles in an earthquake.

Again, he moves. The atmosphere is filled by dust as fine flying ash. The ash covers him. He, with sounds flowing in breathy lights. He breathes and they are chasing one another, orbiting around by cloudy orbs as they appear as spirit forms. They fly by the directions and then fan out. They spin wild orbiting around the cloud of energies.

Deep breathing begins. There is expulsion of the breath that can be heard in the space as letters form, and the cloud of gases are filling divine energy in ideation.

These letters form condensing in the gravity, magnificent spiriting attributes felt, and by these changes they are intended, executed in timed elements.

These miracles form energies that fit the miracle of time by their qualities. Time acts out the season with each change stepped by reason.

It is the time of death and resurrection; the Eastern sky lights in stars, that appear rewarding us with spring and resurrection by their patterning.

The sun will soon rise due east when crossing the equator in perfect equal nights. It is in the spirit point of perfect balance and harmony, centered between the pillars of the Northern and Southern skies, and perfect centered between earth and sky, in the

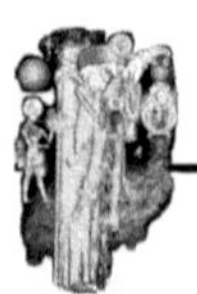

sphere of Beauty at equinox.

It forms the sacred cross, balanced at the resurrection in Tiphareth, the seasons, marking the line between the spring and fall set upon the Tree of Life, where it is moving half toward darkness, and half toward light.

Energies support the equanimity of superconscious energies, by the perfect temple now that is formed, setting still, as the sun moves in a straight course in the perfect line across the sky on the perfect day of "*death and resurrection*" of the year.

The drumming is loud enough to cover movement of his footsteps sent traveling below our footsteps now, in the darkness transforming it with light, to greet us in the night of mortality. Time is masked by it. Again, he stops to rear back and cries out speaking.

Sage Time (Cont'd)

Jubilation, here comes our thought – reforming space vehicles; amassed as One miracle in time, to touch the sacred East, by the bounty of the beautiful!

One miracle in accumulation. This is the culmination of our dreams formed here in pressing thoughts sublime!

Such the condensation gathered there in gravity, forming miracles of Time.

Sage Time fades into the atmosphere and from this begins to appear, in the cloud again, another forming coming into sacred scenes, in which we see low lights shining, on an altar that appears created out of it.

The altar is simple white.

There is music playing lightly keeping time, which changes, changing rhythms periodically, to create a powerful opening in our light.

The twelve members of the council come approaching, each entering as chanting members—each numbered and blessed in their dressing, in ceremonial attire. With the faces painted, they celebrate each member signs. Representing their sign of the zodiac.

They approach the altar, but each comes turning, winding, to set themselves in time by their footsteps, and sit within their places.

Each place assigned to the time and space into which they belong. Being born as creatures. Time created.

They are dressed, decked by their colored symbols, with their faces painted. Each with clear images of celestial features.

In both hands, they carry lighted wands. They glisten without assistance.

In their makeup on their bodies, arms and faces, are metallic and crystalline elemental colors made from precious minerals and the subtle metallic oils, purified and colored in the elements they represent and as charged by prescription.

With rhythmic chants, they appear wild but organized, purposed in their celebration. They address their movements with each degree of their sign, and with each step they unfold their meanings, identified and projected there into the atmosphere.

They are announcing themselves, as they move through their paces, as gods moving—going and returning.

Each movement is calculated by their symbols formed for the waking of their sign. Their walk is stepped in fylfot paces, as if choreographed, for the pendant placement of their limbs and lines, and the presentations, and by the appearances on their faces, and the Great Mystery that is glowing in their eyes.

They breathe the colors of their signs.

These events determine the heart by the ceremonial expressions, forming passions in the mind, and by the spirit of the Archetype that is measured by the depth.

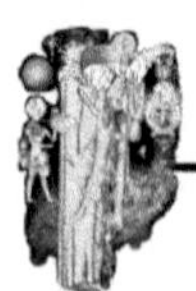

The soul, excited in the Atma-sphere, is there to store the memory, waiting for its time, when its elements may act.

These are time-actors. They are ghostly specters walking slowly toward their sanctioned stations. They "clack, clack" their jeweled wood and metal wands, as if percussion instruments were made lively by their song, and these are all colored in oily metals, and laced in gemstones and metals, in their measured, colored places, that were turned out, and cut, to represent the months, days and hours and merge into their specific times.

These then were formed by imagination and that magic undertaken, by their powers of their signs.

They move only as described, until they greet the altar, and their timed steps meet their ritual obligations, where they are sacred-seated in a circular circumferencing line.

Themselves rigid in their circle, sitting 'round the altar white, and they according to their colors. Their principles markedly rocking now and keeping time.

The Khan Gu appears slowly visible in his station, coming from the invisible silent formless beginning, and he can be seen standing at the altar, in a magical stance of celebration, with arms extended as one form a blessing in the presentation, and by this he meets his obligation of Easter self-sacrifice, as one appearing crucified.

The Myth created, he relaxes with everyone in their places.

He begins to speak out loud before the gathering is together, as if by the moments making, in uttering a prayer and giving the insights of the hour, in the sweetest contemplation.

These *All Elements*, settle into the ritual oration with the subtleties of silent obligations, that speak, breathed in words unspoken by the mind, that is softly beginning being voiced.

Khan Gu

Breath in me, we are one. We dwell within one substance. More than to be consumed in one is to know one. Our thought must be inflamed, our consciousness merged; reflecting One in luster and illumination.

Sacred thought, bring form and substance to our premonitions. Reveal and clarify our impressions intent.

Events hang on dark and ominous clouds that have shadowed our land and people.

Now we lift up our prayers and meditations, for the sacred unveiling of the mysteries enclosed within the hour.

All souls are gathered here for your divine administration awaiting insight coming from thy command.

Attra, a beautiful young lady, is cued and she enters through the temple doors. Prompted, she is followed by many others. She takes her place in her station. The rest follow single file. They continue and are seated beyond the ceremonial sanctuary, in the lower alcove, as the faithful presence before those who have come as their selected audience.

They are seated in a far distance seating, as put away in safe places, away from the ceremonial hierarchy.

This, so as not to disturb the sacred energies of holy places, but by their breath and by their eyes they may contribute to the ceremony with their concentrations, prayers, and meditations, giving form and substance through their sight, projecting conscious breath and superconscious energies, these are sent by their spirit in the form, of concentrated light.

Attra

Arama Atitich, I am come. I carry the sacred implements of our Holy assemblage.

Attra holds up a vessel filled with magical implements and presents these to the Khan Gu on one bended knee. She lays these before the altar and turns around to face the seated assembly, staring at the cover of the ceiling, which clearly is seen as open to the sky, beneath the stars at night, as reminding one of the rooftop at Dendara, beneath Khemetian skies.—All Chants begin.

Khan Gu

Most profound and internal Lord of hosts, we eulogize beyond our greatest admiration.

Let two forms on one, finite and infinite, hail the presence of the Master of the inner world.

Profound wisdom come out of the triumphant silence.

Hail!   KH

Council Members 4-8-12

KH (Guttural breath)

Khan Gu

Hail! A

Council Members 2-10-6

A (Aspirate breath)

Khan Gu

Hail! O

Council Members 1-5-9

O as subtle from the Silent—like an infinite power it moves expanding over mind. These chants occur in succession and hold until the Khan changes the letters by his Word.

Khan Gu

Hail! S

Council Members 11-7-3

S (The dental sound, it sticks like fire or hiss of a snake.)

Khan Gu

Hail living God, host of our living flesh—power of our internal sacrifice.

Hail!   KHa-hA-O-S. KHa-hA-O-S. KHa-hA-O-S. The searing breath.

Hail unto the decade out of the black unity of the infinite internal sphere of night. Hail depth deep and depthless, deathless wherein the gods delight as seen past twilight coming out in night.

Hail unto the brightness of the Kingdom of the Motherland.

Invoke here now the mothers of our beginnings

Khan Gu & 12 Council Members

A-M-S; M-A-S; S-A-M . . . S-M-A; M-S-A; A-S-M

(*A*=Breathy *Haa* - *M*=Silent, mute, expanding, water - *S*=Dental, *Sh*, Fiery.)

Khan Gu

Hail to the six dimensions of the ten infinitudes, supporting spirits on the Tree of Life! We ordain from the beginning infinite to the end. To the good and the ill and unto the heights and depths of time!

And, unto space easterly we praise in adoration of the good, the morning sun revealed by its waking. To the west revered in slumbers.

To the north and south to poles of dark and light in their seasons undertaking. We have come unto the flash in the sphere of the mother light.

Come! Thought wedded to infinity and give birth to forms in living memories!

All 12 Council Members

KH-AA-AH

The throated breath sings to become a strong AH! And the sound continues in the long chant even while Khan Gu is speaking.

The twelve members also begin a rhythmic pounding of the feet as if drumming on their drums, but that drumming instantly ends, when Khan Gu speaks again, though the chant remains soft suddenly, without end while he talks.

Khan Gu

Breath of Life—Soul, will and reformer of water and fire. Wings of the Soul Eagle and First Mother of our Creation. Breath of Life, whose consonants formed the song of the living.

Twilight reverence, revel in their revelation of their

luminous sprites seated in the stars at night still seated past their midnight.

We bow before these graces unseen save by their luminaries: "Ma-Aur-Ra Mayam as the mother lighting the illusion of the sun by day, she is the all-seeing light of Miriam."

Let us raise upon the unspoken wordless, the Word by Thought Mystery, as the infinite and eternal breath.

Create here the Temple of the Glorious, in the joy Tik-koon Aulam.

Evoke the sphere of goodness by the voice light of Yah-Heh- Waum.

Let Being split as Monarch to create into the forms of uncountable generations; be they laid upon the breath and displayed as self-formed combinations for Kings and gods; there poised upon the central flame, as light let them shine upon the fiery atmosphere.

All 12 Council Members

OO . . .

Their voices are first silent but grow to loud and strong, "OO", and this continues chanting while Khan Gu continues speaking.

Khan Gu

We divine now as one becomes two, and splits our holy vestige.

We tear our veil and render in two: spirit and water.

Moisture . . . symbol of our eternal unity, and that emergence into living forms.

We call the angel of substance, and shadow of the breath!

All 12 Council Members

HA – MMM

Loud and strong it explodes from the beginning and their voices continue the chant while the Khan Gu speaks.

Khan Gu

Upon the holy personage, the Great Mother, is given to shine in the powers of assimilation.

Muted sound "-Mmmm-".

HA! Water brought to silence upon the fortress of imitation.

Here, crystalized, cold-formed breath unveil our lovely land upon the fields of Mu.

Dry to dust and air by heat and fire!

MA!

All 12 Council Members

RA - SSHH

Loud and strong voices shout and continue the "sh" chanted while the Khan Gu speaks.

Khan Gu

RA, the soul flame!

SH, the sacral reflected inhabitable throne of glory!

Arama! Founder of the infinite universe!

Arama! The living secret of the ineffable all.

Arama! Alchemical Substance of Reality, thought, and the miracle of the generation of living beings!

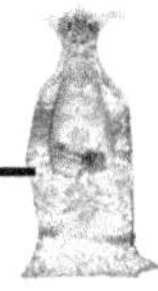

All 12 Council Members

Th-o-th

This long and drawn out each independently with the "Th" which is a soft hissed sound that merges into the silence of the breath as O in unison to begin to form the cloud of superconscious energies by the elements collected with the breath's breathing as the soul of life, and that continues chanting, with each breath softly played, while the Khan Gu speaks.

Khan Gu

Within the center is spun BRaa-Hama

His hard *BR- ahama* breath is breathed into the altar lighting it.

Khan Gu (Cont'd)

From water and air -Aneh-

A-breathy, N-long silent, Eh-breathy . . .

Khan Gu (Cont'd)

Brahma binds the sphere of KH-R-S-N-Ha the infinite elemental name.

Invoke now reality out of nothing!

Call the non-entity into existence!

Bring crystalized forms out of intangible air! THOTH . . . Jyoti! Keh-Ra Djeuty!

All 12 Council Members

TH-O

TH-O is sung as a harmony in unison. All 12 members of the council again begin stamping feet as drums in time wildly while

they chant, and it continues nonstop as they draw out long, the breath continuous, with the letter "O."

Khan Gu

Water thy house of power.

O' Superior to all things!

Hoa- Ana- Atitich!

Hoa- Ana- Atitich!

Hoa- Ana- Atitich!

All 12 Council Members

Hoa- Ana- Atitich!

All stamping of the feet stops. A long silence ensues. Khan Gu slowly continues softly speaking.

Khan Gu

(Softer)

The temple is aflame in thought.

All 12 Council Members

(Softly)

Brahma.

Khan Gu

The council forms as one.

All 12 Council Members

(Softly)

Brahma.

Khan Gu

Beloved guests have arrived. We desire communion.

Attra, bring the visitors before us.

Attra

Beloved Khan, I am the Holy Guardian and Watcher of the Way, why do they approach the temple?

Khan Gu

They shall become the preservation of our tomorrow.

Attra

Then by your will alone, I will provide for their attendance. They may be sworn to silence ere they enter here. All Praise, Khan Gu!

She turns to the outer group and to all she gives the signs.

Attra (Cont'd)

Khan Ha! Khan Ba! Khan Ha BRama!

All stand. She places her right hand over heart in salutation, with left arm forming the 345-right triangle. All respond in kind and are seated.

Attra exits . . . All are silent. She returns with Caanon and Sheea. They each are presented as sworn members, and give right angle salutations as a natural form of acceptance.

The Khan Gu crosses his arms having adjudicated for their admission, and all the council follows suit showing their support.

Sheea

Arama Atitich Khan Gu.

Caanon

Arama.

Khan Gu

Come before the altar.

He speaks extending his hands. It is silent for a long period until the pressure builds and Sheea speaks out of turn.

Sheea

Why have we been called?

The long pause breaks with her voice and she is embarrassed. The twelve members of the council suddenly softly chant in unison, *"Ah,"* and a light music begins as their song is generated . . . this to purify again the atmosphere effected by her speaking.

Caanon

Our meeting in the lab revealed some new . . .

Total Silence. All speaking stops.

All 12 Council Members

La Mayach, La Mayach, La Mayach

Their voices are not in unison, the rule is to Malkata, the gateway to the Kingdom. There has been a vote taken. But having been made it is their final decision. Not one is casting a dissenting vote. They will descend to the pure world below as gate keepers to the Kingdom. Three times each, each would say these to inspire true words. Each word to account for the three worlds. Khan Gu softly speaks.

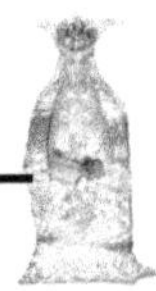# Khan Gu

It is done!

Attra, make the way!

All 12 Council Members

Brahma.

Attra moves forward and she stands before the altar facing the East. She has put on wings of power that extend beyond her arms and appearing as a form of Isis. She is slightly forward of the gathering in the darkness on a high platform midway above their audience and below Khan Gu.

Attra

We are upon a great revelation. May the spirit of thought invisible manifest in the heart. Cleanse us in the spirit formed of divine morality.

There, an image begins to form in the dark space before her. She views this through the cloud with a central fire form. She begins to converse with it.

Attra (Cont'd)

I speak in pledge of Brahma!

San Bra!

San HaMa!

San Ha Brach-Ma! Ama!

Behold Hoa-ana — I stand at the door of Judgement.

Behold my KHA — with arms out-stretched unto the Way. I am the dove ascending; the Ascended.

I am pure — my wings outstretched are unfolded, at the

place of passage, my virtues flying are my sacrifice unto the everlasting gates of Eternal Life.

I am here before you. I am at the portal to pass. I am the witness for those assemble here.

I, call to the central flame;

I, call unto the Island of Brahma!

A light begins to spread in four directions to form a cross within the atmosphere.

Attra (Cont'd)

Hail light . . . Coming forth from the central sphere!

I have sought passage, and come bearing a sealed proclamation. The council has decided.

She holds her hands crossed over the central heart.

Attra (Cont'd)

I have come that the one may open the seal, and reveal the contents unto me.

Attra breaks her form, and with her right arm motions toward Khan Gu.

Attra (Cont'd)

Behold the Khan! Behold Khan Gu!

He stands before the passage with strangers. Hear him.

His heart calls for admittance into the wonders and he speaks for our past and future generations.

She stands rising to his level and circles around the altar as if in flight, and she returns to her place in the front of the altar, with arms outstretched toward Khan Gu, again in a kneeling position,

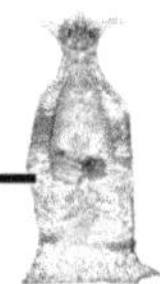

while facing staring into what is now forming in the dark sky, the Isle of the Sacred Eye of Brahma flaming in the light.

Attra bows her head forward with arms crossed in the center of her chest. Khan Gu begins to speak.

Khan Gu

I have attained the power over the steps of the shining ones who light as spirits in the night the brightness of the firmament.

The Lords of the ineffable shine here before me and I am in them and they in me.

I have, even before, ascended the Mountain of the Illuminated and returned to witness the love of this creation.

There I viewed as witnessed from the crest of the peak A-N-EH EL Yon.

I know, even I, the ways of the secret doors of the sacred temple— A-L-O-Bra-Ha-YaEem.

I am the voice of Kre-Esh-Na-Ha!

Ssh-Eh-KR-Eh-Tau HaRa-ARu.

This body of life swears witness to the visions seen within the light.

Ah-EL-O-Ha-Eem!

Ee-Hah-WOo-Heh

Yah-Heh A-Ru!

I prepare the way in me, thus:

That light shines bright in me.

May I arise up again to that spirit of this, the light of

God in me.

Ignite the flaming candle of lights in me,

Along the column of the divine in me.

Here, appearing humbled before that Sacred Eye.

The vision of that vastness witnessed is the archway of that Celestial Archetype!

Seer! Sheer virgin light, delight in me!

May I be granted safe passage before the Temple of Light in Me.

Upon the wings of God send thy messenger of Light to bear witness to my virtues that appear in Me,

Carried to the Lord Seer BeTh-RaMa, here, standing now before me as Attra, the Mother of our Mysteries.

She sees through the visions formed by Mother Attra.

May I be granted power to overthrow my adversities, upon the spirit of Water and Air.

Behold Fire-Spirit, I become the thought of the Golden Eagle delighted in that great space in A-Kha-Sha in the Atma-sphere.

I am born from the center of the Golden Egg.

Behold the opening of the Eye before us assembled here.

Behold the Sacred Eye — Ha-Ra-Aur-Ra!

Come water!

The Soul. Fire in thought—delighted by its motion.

Behold, Ha-Ra-Meh-Se

Behold thought in me!

Come unto the children of the Kingdom of the

Motherland. Pay homage to the generation of Love.

Caanon and Sheea fall as if pushed forward on their knees in front of the altar, facing those members of the audience with arms crossed. In shock they are seated before the Sacred-Seeing-Eye, seeing all by it in their minds, and they flatten to their faces pressed into the ground in adulation.

Attra does the same on a level below them in the center of the two.

A soft gong sounds and the three rise on their knees with arms outstretched.

Sheea

Ha! Ba-Bel, we raise our souls, to praise the Holy tower of our ancestral tithes.

The serpent is lifted unto Ra and the Mother bears fruit for her children. We are here rushed in the spirit of her delight

Caanon

Lift our hearts swiftly who are together raised upon the altar of our thoughts, Za-Ro Za-Du, and feel our flame extended in the sacred fires of moral generations fourfold in wisdom extended in all eight directions. Tza-di is the star, as witness to our perfections.

Love and Peace.

We address the fraternity: Ra! Ma! Glory Ineffable.

Khan Gu

Heirs of Mu, come, in . . . Come unto me. Assume my being.

He brings both hands to the center of his forehead to form a triad with open palms.

By now all twelve are pointing toward Khan Gu, and with their hands are pointing to his forehead, the entire attention of the audience is focused toward him.

Khan Gu (Cont'd)

Transport the self beyond the veil of time.

Enter in . . . your thoughts merging into mine . . . Consecrate the image of virtue into the temple of the Sacred One . . .

Come unto me . . . Come . . . Come . . . into my being.

Assume Self as one . . .

Aum Ma . . . Aum Ra . . . Aum Bara-Aum

EL-Om Ha-Ya Heh-Yah Brahm-Ha

Yah NaRa-NaRaYaNa . . .

They all continue repeating this chanting for a very long period of time. It seems as if hours pass away and then it is naturally faded.

All then join in private mantric chants. These soft, long, slow, low breathing rhythmic chants, chant to themselves as their private prayers are undertaken. The lights are faded dim to darkness and sweet soft sounds of music begins.

As the lights are low on the altar a face begins to form. It is a youthful face that floats above the altar in heavy make-up and symbolic signs. The head moves slowly in the rhythm of the music and the soft voices sighing as the young divine is incarnated in the brightness as the Ever-Youthful-Light.

A cloud is forming as the face begins to take its shape out of that cloud. The altar is in the place of the first state in the Beginning. It glows with a strange new light as the low lights oscillate and flicker, moving shadows up and down that are changing places.

The child slowly shapes into a solid form, as just a face formed appearing out of emptiness, as the reflection of the divine as the Lesser-light-perfection.

An unvoiced discourse begins speaking aloud from the Atma-sphere.

Two voices speak, male and female, speak in unison and give the sense of endless time, passing in endless states by angelic voices. These several voices vary over voices leveled, fading in and out.

In careful movement and subtlety, the voices pass in places shifting left to right moving in space, only slightly and gently, creating motion in the sound waves, by their spirits moving in the space, as they circle between the quarters of the room, and are detectable as space in motion by the inner ear.

Subtle! Undetectable by the sound! These shifting forces move their places as voices stirring waves, within the space that appear with stellar lights, like two voiced choirs speaking simultaneously in the interstellar ABBA-Ba voice one upon the other in speech dreams of vocal acapella.

Interstellar Beings

(A)

Hail . . . Mortal of Earth . . . Meditations . . . have come . . . Void Space

(B)

Hail . . . Mortal . . . Your . . . Thoughts have crossed . . . the . . . Void

(A)

I AM . . . Thought . . . Interstellar . . . Space . . .

(B)

Come from Celeste from . . . Thought I am . . . You ...

(A)

A Planet . . . afar from . . . Remote Galaxy . . . Periods . . . Not of Earth

(B)

. . . My Planets . . . A World . . . Beyond time . . . Not of Earth Period

(A)

Relation . . . Now . . . Is . . . Merged . . . as . . . One

(B)

Time . . . Time Past . . . Future . . . One

(A)

Non-Entity . . . Becomes . . . exists . . . Beyond . . . Space . . . Thought . . .

(B)

. . . Light . . . Cloud . . . Time . . . One . . . Pearls layered . . . in Space . . .

(A)

Mu . . . Will fall . . . Consumed . . . Beneath . . . Waters . . . In fire . . .

(B)

*The great Mother Tree . . . Fruits . . . Aflame in . . . Her
Love . . .*

(A)

*Eastern . . . Mountains . . . Preserved . . . High
Mountains Remain . . .*

(B)

*Mountains to South . . . and . . . Central . . . Must spread
to . . .*

(A)

*Gautama . . . known tomorrow . . . Yu-ca-tan . . . Indies .
. . Andes . . .*

(B)

*Continents . . . Tribes will divide . . . Ignorance . . . To
above Waters . . .*

(A)

*There will . . . come . . . to . . . rise . . . in . . . Akkadia . . .
East . . .*

(B)

. . . Marsh . . . lands . . . as Aztlan . . . Waters . . .

(A)

*In Marshlands East across Mountains, North, West,
South and east.*

There is a short pause. Transitions build on tension that increase with time in the formation of a massive cloud of superconscious energies, as the entire crowd creates the form united in one thought. Voice "A" continues speaking.

(A Cont'd)

Great colonies of Mu will lie fathoms deep ever removed from the eyes of her children.

Her lights will fade into the sea with her crafts . . . her achievements will become shadows unto the living memory of her royal habitation.

Become immortal . . . (echo).

Speech, thought and dreams need spread into the lands east and west and to points high upon the horizon.

Take with you the provisions of thought and creation, with your insights for invention. Find your sacred place as ordered in creation, dependent on the rotational movement of Earth, then rest in those places suited to your natures on its axial lines, and by their division on the ecliptic plane across the zodia, and sort these above and below the horizon, and circumscribe and divide these, by their directions, layered within space between the atmosphere and the Atma-sphere.

Build vessels made to hold manifold preparations to sail or fly upon the elements over earth, water, air and fire.

Inspire these with works by their appearances, traits and characteristics and sort them by their signatures of personality and self-awareness, for initiation and the ideal forms for new beginnings.

Determine by these travels finance, wealth and properties. Cultivate growth in these divisions through

the character, the substance and the values as a measure of self-worth and those powers of possession.

For comfort, communicate these between the neighboring tribes as found between and within the relations of the homes and families. On your journey, find time for pleasure, recreation and leisure; for the times of love, romance and self-expression.

Create the foundation for the house of health, and discover the roots of self-determination, liberty and freedom. Serve them and govern by these in binding tasks and duties, skills and training, required for the proper employment of the people of the kingdom, and to give them comfort for their necessary care.

Build partnerships, close confidantes and marriage relationships for peopling the earth, and unite bonds in commercial partnerships developing creativity as the aegis of diplomacy. Beware of warring classes and tribes and those who live to murder and demoralize.

You shall govern the comings and goings in all incarnations between the world of mortality and lives lived for the immortal life, by following the legends of both birth and death, and all those subtle tendencies that exist beyond, but formed the earth.

Serve others faithfully and provide for the fitness of society.

Become builders and create the House of Philosophy not alone for divinity, but to model these insights into religion and government, to establish the rules of ethics and authority for the public good, and to deter the worlds enmity of differences.

Establish the Orders in Society, for the tempering of ambitions, motives and careers; for tradesmen and the

clergy, and for the saints and sages who will come and go. Establish cultural institutions for higher learning, religion and philosophy and associations for public unity.

Gather together those of like-mindedness to collaborate in wisdom. These may find benefits to fulfill their hopes and wishes.

Set aside time for the Mysteries of self-knowing, inspired by the oneness with ethical study in order to serve divinity.

There should be places for those as well who commit atrocities against society that they may be tempered, and taught to govern themselves more wisely, and moreover to punish those who should be punished.

Build hospitals for caring and for birthing, and along with these places for quiet privacy. These places should all motivate those who serve in the welfare of self-sacrifice, and the giving over of one's comforts to follow dreams and assist others.

Order by their angles, timed practices in initiations that are varied, weighed, and weighted, according to their elements and the temperaments. Establish these acts according to those things fundamental, immovable, or changeable.

Sort these all by the Order of the Great Name of God and set these according to their domicile, or by their rule beneath the Sun, Moon and those qualities determined by the stressed energies of atmosphere and Atma-sphere, in their divisions of Time.

And, create days of celebrations for their consideration in consciousness, space and times by the hours of the day, days of the week, and months of the year, for the times set aside for remembering one's relationship with

divinity. These shall be your Temple functions dedicated to Time. Develop these to inspire your sciences so they do not fall into egotism.

First, make your preparations to conduct migrations, for establishing for the means for remembering the virtues for building nations, that are set to move either toward the east, or western continents—to prepare those in great difficulties to cross vast mountains, forests, valleys and tropical places without the cause for erring.

Calculate your positions among the stars along with the sun and moon's positions, by building Obelisks as astrolabes, and reading these by the weeks, months, days, and hours to determine the aspects of Time's intervention for the best migration, for taking every moment's passing, in order to reach your destination safely and unobstructed.

Move quickly in order to preserve the culture by the bits gathered now, to shape your practices along the way. These will inspire the soul's identity or that foundation of material clay, for the social, intellectual, emotional, and soul's enrichment.

Make ready the youth of the tribes whose long journey should carry with it the weight of their tomorrow.

Time draws near when her sovereign queen Mother shall be swept asunder by the tides. The angel of light with her bright eyes, will fall with her fruit under the degradation of her fires under SH-Tau-Nu, the fire of the cross, before the coming of the new Moon and her dark night of Shiv-Ra-Ta-Re.

Races will cherish her memory, but the aggravation of time, and the ill anger of her children, will cause the mother to fall a greater fall; taking with her the real fruits

The lights in the temple fade and the images disappear in darkness and silence. An eternity passes.

Chapter Four

Sage Time

Peradventure, it is set! The vision of things of heaven have now become manifest in the Mother-light. Fortunes by their fortune sign off to dark defeats. To La Mayach, but as history will witness it, it will turn daylight into night, as the world rolls over suddenly.

On sojourn, Time, unceasing; determines the fate of those who are sending off their future progenies into desert wastes of mortal hells. To live in forests and jungles and to travel across vast deserted plains.

Almost naked as the animals. Each by each becoming mortal enemies. So, there is much to learn before this.

God conceived. The plan unfolds behind the scenes waking havoc as these divine creatures who have already fled.

Concealed, the Director and Master of the play concedes to forgone futures. They are spirits of the future, and need to get back to it, but for now they leave this state of futurity by the will of Providence, and he lets nature's matron now conspire with him, for the betterment of these, on the path of initiation.

She is the Mother of Memories, and so she now binds with them, with their walking through her remembrances, pretending, portending in the future that she does not exist, in that shadowy state of subconsciousness, when they will be lost to mortal

senses.

Her gods have all turned out in nature in celebrations. They inspire us by their juices, and they give life vitality in vegetation. These gods determined the narrow fates of her creatures, by assisting virtues in their food. Providing healing properties.

By her release, these powers entered into their centers everywhere. By the suggestive call, the magnetic powers are born electrical in their movement, for the integration of these by gravity, holding together the mortal form.

These all, are occupied by breath weaving in and out, timed in phase and frequency. To see into these, we must first look deeply in meditation, into the body, through our imagination. We are as puppet dolls.

The divine descendants of the gods conceiving, are seen entering into these bodies of mortal forms. In these they communicate their needs and determine their functions, and support their creation, sustenance and deaths, from the atom to the cells and organs.

The gods by each with each said, "This is mine. My Body. My Blood. My Flesh." For those who enter, they have simply come to pay their debt by this. We serve in faithfulness, Time and the Lord to do our duty by this.

They came out into the shadows of mortality, and poured their properties into stems, roots, stalks and leaves for building, and for glory designed some with flowers blossoming, and some by these before the fruit, and blessing thus the food and vegetation.

The new eyes of Man glowed in tempered thoughts revealed by these vitalities of the gods, and the soul

was no longer unexposed. It shone through their mortality. Behind those shadowed walls, the soul now is seen as lighted before dark spaces, and there it is tested by these shadows of hidden memories. As each is brought to witness these new realities, caused by falling into form.

Lit in lights beneath the stars at night, and by the lighted elements that follow by the day, and seen by shades of good and evil natures, they have no less shown little to nothing of themselves.

First, they hide as creatures in the shadows in fear of everything.

Things meant well, were beginning to go wrong, as all things subject to nature they break down, and this was discovered at the point of failure in the fall into mortality.

These all, are parts played in acting roles staged for lifetimes cycled by their soul. In these, with age, the good is slowly covered over, by light and shades of elemental flesh.

Sadly stated, these creatures became the living graveyards of composting carrion. Born into those fields supporting bacteria, and from vegetation the peat, salts, silt and clay; trapping mineral particles in water and atmosphere.

Once the breath is pumping they are born into the mines of earthen elements, taken from the common properties of the earth's outer crust.

They churn as life within the blood in forming the living qualities as the ceramic plastic crystal dolls engineered into flesh and blood.

Beauty is now seen in this mass covering through these sad new features. It exhibits, moves and travels with all the challenges of the soul, mind and vitality, through youth, growing to old age. Their changing times are captivating and they begin to write songs about their changing temperaments.

The spacious scene of divine imagination becomes as ignorance falling into form, creating their lasting personalities in character, but arraigned as prisoners of the flesh.

Reflecting Life in imagination, it was made more difficult by it, being weighed down by gravity and death.

Conceived between heaven and earth, these living gods entered, reborn as mortal-immortalities who were not wasted as those lounging in long dreams or fantasies, but were born into living flesh as sentients!

Damned, for the long path backward, toward cause of liberation. These shadow spirits now are determined to make the journey on that long winding back, along the up and down, by these winding elevations, being clever, rising/falling, on the bidding of the guardians of the mysteries of La Mayach, to serve and challenge them.

God in Life is seen as pleasure seeking. The real exposed for its shapes as mysteries forgotten in geometries, as the reality is revealed only by letters and their numbers.

Freedom cannot be undertaken. Where they once lived in the wordless unspoken thoughts, they are silent, now numbed by senses, that bring on the glimmer of false peace of mind.

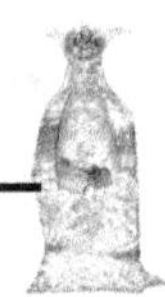

There are lessons to be remembered. These subjects now lost to forgetfulness.

They journey now with us is to mark nature's treasure find.

Called back to virtues, these old thoughts appear in the fog of unrememberances—passing on in those lost subjects for generation after generation. Living on fruitful fertile mountain fruits and berries, and planting coastal valleys, and the fields across plains. They huddle by surrounding deltas in huts built by the bays. By these they are happy to play, eat and breathe, while they raise their families.

They are all asleep in senses satisfied for dreaming daily, in their comfort of clay, with hearts beating time, embracing mortal forms.

Gone, thereby the cascade of immortal comforts, that followed once like the lighted waterfalls, for these ancient seekers. They now are flying fast and turned to false ways. Unable to find their subterranean life in that immortal ocean's water main. Immortality appears lost, in the vast stream of consciousness.

Time is changing but they remain. They are left behind.

Toughed out, when starting on this new adventure, they will soon confound the tilling grounds, and bear abuse in dryness, before there comes wetness to witness soggy rains.

Fields will be filled with trees felled with deep roots left behind, and those sad plantings, will be lost by over watered drenching, or creatures that devour them.

So, dredging will be necessity for these flooded fields

once they are filled with grain. The harsh realities of heat and cold will begin to set upon them.

The wiles within life's challenging, will be supporting them in Time, by destinies recovering difficulty.

The forged waterways of life conforming, will drain into elemental streams, where fresh waters will delight between dry famines, and the flooded wells, so they shall set aside canyons for reserve. No more feasts of plenty, but enough.

Alone, we shall consider them seeing their faces in their futures. Named, then nameless, falling between cycles repeating in rebirthings. They may be seeing old friends renamed, as little swaddling entities cuddled in their cradles.

The unborn, yet unwilling, but ever-living, returning again to farm and cultivate. Such will be the fate of wealth and poverty. While taking respite only for the moment, between these twins of birth and death.

The will? The Will, it will be revealed as the cause for being cycle-born. The Will states, be trapped or be initiated. This is life's inheritance.

To perceive our lives, we relive inspired by the metaphor. The drenching vital chain of Nous will fall down through the vital mind, and bring the sense of freedom through visions of imagination.

Shining on mind, the sightless glass, before the wise, Khan Gu, his spirit seeing eyes unconcealing future acts, regardless, they are proceeding. These lessons are now set down as future facts, to pacify the fates.

This light bearing seed is now designed for creating their fate and future progeny. Set down clearly by

those sent down from Mu.

Here they sprout fair poetic words and deeds, and with the weeds they scattered books and pages of forgone memories that are predetermined prophecy. These are recorded and sent out before windblown acres' as would garden seed to pass by the water main of superconsciousness.

The fields by gusts of gale recede. The good laws concede, while our new fortunes are born as misfortune. They bear out our destiny in calumny against the Word spoken by divinity.

The plains break before the cloudless waste of dryness. There, will migrations come before tomorrow's death determination.

The sun, Solei seemed to read ahead for prophecy, to see the tests before them. For the sons and daughters of the Sun and Moon, were born out of the land before they rowed across the big seas.

Tastefully, in search of wordy catechism she is there to ensure their fate is not so dreary when it is undertaken. She and Khan Gu . . .

Seen in their challenge, God's starry staring lights, beam down from heaven, and they return the stares between earth and heaven as two subjects face to face. Before our light defines the shapes to come when the hour approaches.

God disappears into a blazing memory in the receptors of sense mortality. There the blind form searches for the subtle state of wisdom.

To gaze upon such a foolish world ahead. The dark and light, fair-mixed energies between valleys and

such mountain air are as seen by these must mingle.

Between earth and sun, the God no longer revealing that presence that is everywhere, once embracing everyone, is now just a fire in the starry atmosphere.

Face to face, our lifetimes are seen as within the vision singled out by the Stone of Love. Now the stars no longer appear as gods seen in their bold powers in the night.

These will be witnessed only by their starlight. The wars of heaven will mean nothing. All will be disordered chaos in the mind when the senses come to life at midnight.

Awake! Lamb awake, before the slaughterhouse, to reel before the song to remember bliss, with that gentle "Baa!" Before they come to take the flesh.

Reveal the Word, Ba-Ra-Bara-Se-Ta to call down the light, glowing from the beginning AL-HaMa, and then call down the Word from heavens Shem-Sham-Mayim, as the "Great-Name-there-by-the-Waters" falling down from paradise meeting earthen madrigals for poets and for saints.

Birthing, live the kind voiced, and with that mantric seed, delighting in one another. The Life bleeds the blood rent sacrifice in Am-N-Ra Nama, by the solar power-cause.

Evoke Yah-Me-Nu, of the sexes through Sun, Moon, watery atmosphere and Earth!

To you, here who have come before me, you are these two, the lifetimes of Canaan and Sheea, long past remembering. Dressed for the age of Kali Yug, representing ancient orders.

Depend upon the Word Mystery. Face love, dear echoed, by this new air breathed to sucking lungs.

A Harmony concealing, dangling vibrant life indefinitely.

Damned! You? Yes, perhaps.

Master puppet, mortal life, look and see the puppet doll survives.

To reach for truth become it. Climb away.

Away? Not away! Find the spirit of life and call it back. To recall it here again when we come. Puppet doll, returned to witness you. See that you deserve it!

Make way, there will always be another place to pass, another mile to far surpass, by these spaces walked before these challenges are removed by wondrous days.

Their earthly trials cast earthly miles past, their dye to die cast away like iron casts, with bodies and mass graves these all are cast away like memories.

Sprouting seed? Deathless Mystery returning daily, tis you or I repeating. I am you and you are me.

I plead, breed mortality, and forward cast the line, and tie it to that distant shore, before the life you are about to lead, unless with each new life, should, with the tide, the boatman will come to take your boat away.

The farthest line cast, is that mortality cast away, through that salvation by liberation.

The more breathed, then bodies breed. We gain! Returned. Fortunes lost and won, and generations following one another proceed yet one by one.

Not separated. Then or now. For the farther flung are

not cast away. This sorrow is bred repeating new by merely losing memory. But it is not free of consequence.

All things have their lifetimes and cycles of return. All!

Creatures, plants, animals, energy, stars thoughts, emotions, vitality and man. They revolve, not according to the law but they are bound to turn and revolve around their centers, to circle their tonic or beginning.

Come again liberation! Return there as well.

But there are long ages waiting. There salvation sits just an inch away as Aeons in their making.

Swear by silence to be its guardian, there is silence in liberation, and discover meditation, or the long sleep in contemplation.

But love, truth, honor and virtue first, for doing what's right is righteous.

Now, it is done. We recall our past histories on earth, and the lives living concerting social breeds bred on this mortal plane.

Aghast! Call out the Name! Upon the Tree that spirit sings. The Voice is moved unto the echo that is mirrored by the sun.

Beneath in the root of earth partake with morning, the spirit breaking prayers with the dawn, made new before and then flying beyond the sun. That by day its heat may turn us.

And by night, there, the moon walks through the sky tracing patterns high above us, as it moves on steadily, disappearing monthly, as the opening and closing of

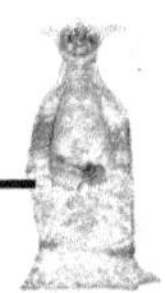

swift changing shapes, transform the appearances by nights. And then repeating and repairing.

To gain therefrom, we call down the spirits. For less is lost and more is won. These are trials for everyone.

These tribulations. These heirs, there they are! They are coming. No-thing is beyond them. Sent forward is the call that was held, waiting on you to come again to pay for them.

Walking forward. Loving futures. To someday become those caring nations centered in that gravitation. We together transcend as spirit to this future drawn from that morality.

Bhur! Bhuvah! Suvahah!

To that vision Tat Savitur Veregnum,

The supreme intelligence . . .

So to the future. It is done. I've said enough.

Upon some inquiry, our soul asks, "From what strange contemplation, this inner principle, could we have better expressed that first form of nature, as in the light of their revelation in this last prescription, in our moral contemplation?"

Upon the visible world, we view the children of nature; parented by representatives of light.

The father, the light of fire, the sun.

The mother, the being whose breath became the living womb of living thoughts; the visible earth—the nurture of living sustenance.

You are the fire, breath and meaning!

One thought generated into the center of the earth.

Come out of the shell O' Mortal!

View the passage of thought between your neighbors, soon to find their passage and their liberation!

Invoke here, now, the power spoken upon the wind!

Your heart flames in exaltation!

Joy is manifest in being!

Come unto me all who weary, your joy shall rest in my pain!

Ya-Heh-Wau!

Come unto me.

I am the guide.

There, follow, we go unto the secret way. Cast now the net to forecast our future fate.

Here, the Mystery becomes manifest!

The Sage Time turns and throws head and hand forward and we hit the image with strobing lightning and thunder follows before our imagination, as the scene appears with dialogues that transition into form.

When moving our imagination in time, as in this speech, this now is broken into dream and celebration. As we step into the temple and witness all assembled to make for their education.

Solei

It is consciousness, listen carefully, this is the key to the entire art locked within the center of the circle . . . So unto the changes of heaven time distorts . . .

Caanon

But to what product? What is the outcome?

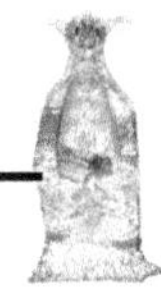

Solei

Consciousness from Superconsciousness is a product of time, transitions of change and the dynamics driven between vibration, motion, orbits and gravity. These are likened to musical elements.

Time is seated between the change. It is beyond the thing as the power that lies in Purusha, the basis, or the cause seen, in the spirit of Sacred Man.

Hold to the memory. Were it not for sacred man, this Cosmos would fly into oblivion! Its gravitation is to the center or tonic element as it is implied in creation.

Caanon

If all is eternal ...

Solei

(She begins tapping on the floor with her long staff slowly and rhythmically.)

Discern the difference? Listen between the interchange of forces, in the power that points between the tones that ring from my sacred staff.

Change is evident. It determines the direction. In music it is that fortune found in the directions pointing between the notes or tones. The future into which you are drawn is the active principle and the past the passive principle.

Sound is manifest in time, keyed to distinct patterns and arrangements that call out the melody by these directors of change.

There is the music of the spheres.

There is the secret to Time generation which draws the elements to itself, self-creating. It forecasts its destiny as it is drawn into its first cause archetype.

There is continuation in motion, within the center of a sphere, in that point that is everywhere and nowhere.

But within the law time exists as consciousness spirited in the interchange of motion in energy. As we reach the pinnacle of the law, the law exists outside of chance or possibility and extends into the ordinance of all things imaginable.

Time consciousness is conceived in the seed of divine invention.

All things are born One, whole and conceived through progeny for the replication into future generations. It need only create once in duality, splitting, for the endless stream to elevate to support its natural needs.

Therein all thoughts are Eternal and boundless, first caused, first forms, in their inclusive consciousness. Thus is the law designation: OOO!

(Spoken as a silent breath.)

Sheea

But the present . . .

Solei

Past and future are present in the God of Time as in eternity . . . Time is motion, change, orbit, gravity and vibration. It is the miracle of Super-conscious dreaming as creative pure intelligence that is omniscient.

Has this satisfied you?

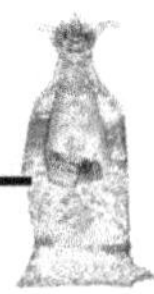

Caanon

My feeling is my head should fly apart . . . but I am not defeated. My first love is to accomplish, the second to rest.

Sheea

Solei, by nature our minds are encompassed around by these transfigurations that travel between heaven and earth, life and death, but the completion of our ideal, bears exhaustion in exaltation. We are comforted but extremely inspired to exhaustion in the bliss.

Solei

Each day comes increasingly closer to the time of submergence and collapse. We must find the path towards our destination as these breaks will soon begin. They have prepared vessels for your quick escape but even these have limited resources and there is no way to replenish what is lost. You will have to make it with the best that you have at your disposal upon leaving. All manufacturing will be lost.

Caanon

The lands are torn half under already. I sense the grounds beneath my feet in vibrations and there are cavities felt that are ready to slip away.

There is stress everywhere and no time to waste.

Sheea

I wish father were here. His peace gave us confidence.

(pause)

Caanon

His transition was honorable. He shall be welcome to sit in the council of our ancestors, as you will one day. But we have to make way. For the moments that are quickly passing away.

Sheea

Time distorts my imagination. I had thought so confidently a year ago.

Love can only imagine, as we did then.

Caanon

It's been a long year for all of us. So many have already fled leaving everything, and they either fell into the world or left for higher places. We are tasked by the council to ensure our wisdom will survive.

Solei

We have no time for this.

Name those forces and powers that are One. Caanon . . .

Caanon

A point or absolute center. What is One is absolute even though they are in two classes One. Each undivided though outward and inward, subtle and gross, of the earth and beyond it. One is the Universal the other the One Nature undivided and omniscient.

The One itself is in opposition to the None or Zero

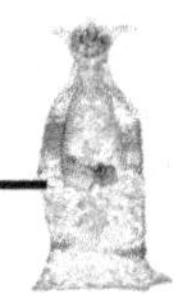

self-identified by that Awareness before the beginning, as entity and nonentity, in luminosity endless and unrequited or One-Sided.

The Universal is the one that is found in unity, union, universe—the elements that are uniform, unifacial, unified, or the sounds distinct, but in unison, the spirit of what is unique and unanimous.

The One Nature undivided, is the all in one before beginning, of every kind, as in the powers that are omnipresent, omniscient, omnipotent, omnigenous or the energies that are absolute in momentum, or omnibus, and as creature Omnicorporeal, omnified and omnifarious as the God of gods that is ominous.

Solei

Two? Sheea . . .

Sheea

A Line. The division divided and polarized. The deva as evolving in separation. To DIV signifying to separate as the Ten is divided between the four and six, between the elements and planetary gods, or the deity from omnipotence, by that power of diversity in the creature, plants animals, man, stars, suns, planets, moons and gods.

Two forces forever in opposition are winding, turning and unturning between the centers, in and out, and to the endless in and the universal out, winding and unwinding by their directions interposed but uncontradicting in their duality, that which is, from that which is not.

This is the contradiction of the unseen by the seen,

the unknown by the known, the unheard by the heard, unfair by the fair, unfelt by the felt, the unrooted by the rooted or the bearable by the unbearable . . . each sharply contrasting by their nature as opposites or antithesis.

That D-I-S is that D-I-V appearance, as the root is to persuade and dissuade, that integrated versus that disintegrated, as those who are contrary by nature.

Solei

Three? Caanon

Caanon

By three we mean to integrate between the two. Each thing first appears by the number three. In creation by the trinity, in causes father, mother, child.

The triad consists in nature of two causes one active the other passive that produce a force in motion in evolution and a dynamic that is experienced between them, either to elevate or fall. A triangle of three angles and three lines on a single plane.

These are those things that are, or that exist in existence. We pay homage to these trinities in the sciences of creation for determining creative causes and roots, by their scope in philosophy and reason.

Solei

In Virtues? First, what is human excellence or the noble quality?

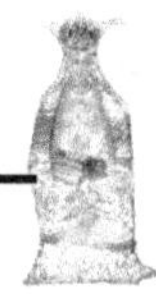

Caanon

Virtue is the regulation of love and service done in silence and the remembering of God in all our peace and happiness. Forgetting oneself in the support of one's personal conceit.

In politics and social interaction, it is loving virtue as that beauty above all things, abhorring silliness and those unwilling to engage in moral learning, but instead have true desire to learn the skills of honor and refinement and all things that are incorruptible, and those who would be examined to be perfect on review or through meditation, in the knowledge of Truth and the enjoyment of its wisdom.

Virtue is awakened in the light of reason and discrimination, for assuming and acquiring those skills deemed worthy, for taking before the seat of Providence for demonstration.

All science falls into evil company without True-Philosophy, where by it, the ingrate becomes as a self-conceited lover, and the ungrateful sells off its credibility for a degenerate price.

It is said that the glory of the family and the Motherland are even greater than paradise. But even greater than these is the honorable reputation.

Where religion holds fast as the true wisdom of society, it must be both that freedom and a bondage yoked to common sense.

Who would be unbound is no more than the fool who has possessed his boat and guards it jealously, and has become so possessed of it that in jealous possession, he escapes the shore without company,

and leaving without a path or map and without spares for oar or engine, or even the trouble of an anchor, he simply sails to expire from the place.

They become the boat and boatman lost at sea with no direction, and they are moved by winds and waves in every direction, until the occupant discovers death as the only way to leave the prison they have made.

Virtue is recalled with the memory of Good Name. Virtue is the root, if God is the blossom, as these are found out in thoughts, words and deeds only by their actions.

Solei

Sheea, how are these noble qualities made beautiful?

Sheea

In the realization of the beautiful beings in the world, where geometries are concealed and revealed in the godly or the sainted sages, in the skillful by their arts, science and engineering and in the temperate by their ability to maintain the peace.

These refine the spirit in the powers created in consciousness as hope, love, peace and happiness. Equally the beauty seen in chivalry and self-sacrifice.

Virtues fight off evil tendencies with the cultivation of purity in thoughts, speech and actions, and these qualities thereby permeate all activities on the spiritual journey from here to liberation in peace, non-violence and love.

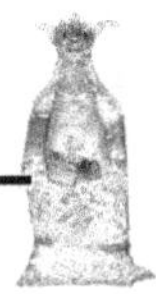

Solei

Caanan, how can man cause these powers to come to life within the personality?

Caanon

By the powers of goodness, truth, and mercy. By the removal of suffering in others and oneself and by the establishment of what is good.

We rely on chivalry as the seal of valor, courage and heroism to make up the spirit of the best. In learning these powers come to life by the practice of reason and discretion.

There are three things that are entrusted to be united before any good may come, and the first is to think well with thoughts true and tested, the next to speak well with words chosen wisely, and the last to act well by those actions representative of these refinements.

To think, know, speak and act according to the Wisdom that is God, is the first cause in creation grounded in the heart. That is the true spirit of the righteous cause.

To learn to speak, see and think no evil is the practice of those who display the greatness that is becoming of a person.

In truth, honesty, and silence, these three provide the path for accomplishing the great good in knowledge, good deeds and gentleness in all things pleasing to every action they perform.

Some good result is due to the will inspired by inner promptings, but one cannot fulfill the desire without a plan which can guarantee success, when that desire is developed in the deed.

For the ideal to be truly realized God must first be encountered as the planner that is installed as the creative workman in the heart, and the conscience must be clear and purified.

Solei

How then are these to strengthen one against the actions of the world?

Caanon

Represent the Truth to guard against the false. Represent peace, love and serve human goodness. God alone represents what is true therefore live a life willed by the realization of divinity.

We may stand firm by seeing the quality and the beauty found in Truth, witnessing what lies beneath the veil that hangs low, cloaking falsehood, and there see clearly discerning the ends of both Truth and Falsehood, and the directions by which their outcomes tend.

No one honors what is false and the person lies when their lives are unfulfilled in deceit and injustice; live for what it judicious, live with honesty and integrity by weighing every action before it starts.

The human body is the shrine in which the Divine is the indweller and representative. We start there first, where it is seated in the central heart supplying the energies of the duality of the Golden Mean, transferring its energies to the right and left, by the two directions flowing opposite and shaped by Ra and Ma.

It is a duty owed to ourselves to listen attentively, modestly and discretely, and then judge others kindly, while keeping as our rule and guide our obligations to our

duty, adhering to our good conscience, and by witnessing what is truth in our actions; following the obvious path that will avoid all misery, and allow ourselves to become inspired by rendering our lives to follow the laws of God. We are only encouraged by that.

Solei

Sheea, how will this ensure our happiness if God is to be found?

Sheea

Love is God, God is Love. There it is simple to see where it is rooted in the heart. In good behavior, this is lived out in our deserving habits, good thoughts, good deeds, good company and with social affability, friendliness and patience as seen supported by our tolerance and restraint, open-mindedness, and life lived in moderation, or through the purification of our desires.

By this we must live in truth, peace and generosity, for these are the godly attributes as gifts in actions recognized and seen when forgiving those who have wronged us, by improving what can be improved of any wrong, and refraining from dealing out our own injustice, by removing ego, pride, passion, envy, or that jealousy that desires to covet what is another person's right.

Herein is the justice born of God and Righteousness. We must first stand firm and protect the innocent. Stand firm against tyranny. Support justice and engage in the community as a messenger of truth, teaching by our actions and not by words alone.

To do that we must know what the truth is first and then live by it. It is of no use to shout out our ignorance. No good can come of it.

Solei

What may we take as our reward from this then?

Sheea

Our true possession is love. Love is the bond that binds the world, the natural possession, and fruit born from the fruit bearing Tree of Life from its centers. That is the only fruit that is made for our eating.

Universal love comes as the only possession that we may garner from the wise, by their lawful acts of goodness.

We should adhere to the gifts of the world's sufficiency, by accepting what that is, by recognizing the right conditions associated with our rewards and how they are achieved, and appreciating the divine gifts from God in this life, and from this acquire the attributes of character, that follow through in this life and in the life to come.

From these practices, we may learn patience from the unfortunate, reflection from the sage, and broadmindedness from the reformers of truth.

These powers imply pursuing our strength of character. By this we must always determine to become the strong and just, the valiant and the merciful—and follow goodness taking the lead that transforms our lives, becoming generous without shame or repentance, even in the sight of affluence or the influence of prosperity.

We may enjoy that experience of reward seeing the joy in profits, honor and the blessings in others, for the ease of good conscience, in the felicity of gracious giving, and those practices that lead us to wealth without end—and this without pride, without untruth and without envy, as our friends kept are honest, and our goal the embodiment

of righteousness.

First learn to speak honestly, saying, "I am the good and righteous person," and then you can learn to follow it, and take heed of its instruction, when the opportunity comes for living love, with unity of purpose and conviction, inspired by the life that is imperishable.

Wealth is like water. Enjoy it. Drink it as needed. Be sure that it is kept clean to avoid contamination.

(Pause)

There is a moment of silence. Then the members of the Council are paraded in and seated. They are quiet. They have come to examine Caanan and Shea to see if they are prepared to defend themselves and stand against the test of time.

Solei

Council begin.

Council Member #1

We are the microcosm developed out of the macrocosm. What does that mean? When we gaze upon the created world and peer out into the universe, these pathways of consciousness are reflected powers and principles that pass between our lives.

These are deeply inherent within ourselves in the shadow of our existence.

The arrangement of universal ideals between the divine gods and stars that shine upon our occult doctrine, pass through each world inspiring the realm of intelligent correspondences. These are subtle but recognizable.

Cosmic powers descend from the gods and move

through us, and they fuse our faculties and energies. These meld energies in our organs through direct relationships to these universal principles and archetypes, in our first cause principles or ideals.

Our ancient teachings teach that Nature is an invisible spirit in its primitive form. That is a breath, whose nature is humble, patient and resolute.

Upon the advent of the breath's appearance seven principal laws and agencies are established.

By our alchemy, its principle form is seen in the hot aqueous gas of the water-breath. The vapor composes the being, the wisdom and the power. Its nature is sulfurous and reflected in the properties of organic acids and essences; the spirit of the living thing.

Solei

From this principle, there is next the establishment of things acidic that are severe, solid, cold, harsh, sharp, and tart or sour; producing covetousness in ignorance and kind empathy in illumination.

This is that medicine supported in the formative power and first principle of the fire. Its strength rests in darkness, on the side of severity.

Council Member #2

From this emerges the motion, vibration, cycle, orbit and gravitation on which the latter depends. In this rests the pain of the transference of the bitter to the sweet. In ignorance, it exists as envy; in the illuminated, it is the desire to do good. This is the second principle of fire which exists in darkness.

Council Member #3

From this is derived the heat of fear and thermal activity, and therein also the sensibilities.   In darkness, it exists as rage, in illumination it exists as tenderness. This is the third generation of fire and it exists in darkness.

Solei

From this emerges the Sun, the central fire of Life and the seed emblem of generation. Being, half in darkness and half in light, it is the Universal Creature. It is the essence and goal of separation, the fourth principle, and the true nature of Arama and the nuclear cleft mission of self-regeneration.

There are three suns to concern ourselves:

- The sun in the heavens, the central form of the father and mother of all creation.

- The sun in the heart, Yam, Yah, Yod, that brings life to every cell and love to every center.

- The sun in the earth which exists as the universal gold as the animate Stone that is ever-living, in the absolute center of the miracle to guard the Liberated Living from coming to that state of inactivity.

In ignorance, the sun exists as egotism and vanity, in illumination it exists as humbleness.

All things are born out of love. Love is the creator, created in love as both first and final form. This is the central principle around which the others revolve. It is in truth the first and last.

Council Member #5

The fifth principle is light, love, and fire, which burns in the oil of mercy over the table of self-sacrifice; the place wherein the heavenly life consists. Its state is chivalry. In ignorance, this exists as vulgarity, in illumination as chastity and is the righteous morality. It is the flight of the imagination upon the Wings of Eternity—the Fire that lights the virtues of the Self.

Council Member #6

And thus, we come to the circle of power, from the light of life. Listen carefully, for in this the Word Miracle is fulfilled in cognition, sounds, and the sacred voice and the hearing into the tones of nature. Thereby the Word of God is revealed as omniscient and omnipresent.

Concentrate and meditate upon these great powers, for they are the extension of the Self.

In darkness, this exists as the shrewd and sly manner, in deceit, craftiness and skill. In illumination, it is the vast wisdom itself.

Solei

Being... Its nature comes from the six emanations of fire. Fire that devours in darkness and fire that glows radiant as that brightness in the light. This is self-conceived. This is as vast as the length, width and breadth of Super-consciousness itself.

In ignorance, the Being exists as sensual desire, in illumination it is the flesh glowing in the vitality of the light, or the virtue of the Body of Light in illumination. God's light that is written into sound:

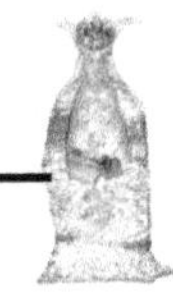

KH-R-SN-A!

Bra-Ah-EL-Oh-Ha-Eem

Yah-Heh-Wo-Heh

Bram, Aum, Lam, Wam, Ham, Yam

Yam, Ham, Wam, Ham . . .

These are the seeds of spirits moving in the light.

It is extremely important for you to understand how to move these wonders of the seven Mysteries, rising from within you as God living in the light. Without them the arts are useless. These are rooted on the path upon the Tree of Life.

With them you will have mastery over the elements of nature, for they are the essence of all existence.

With them all the world will remain in balance. They are the lights shining in the natural formation that is rooted by the Tree of Life.

These are the celestial powers which are unaffected by natural fire or cold, or whether these are challenged by the natural elements that are dry or moist.

They are the seven united, which split and become five in all.

From out of this essence comes first Air, then water; these turn upon one another, and thus the fire is born in nature Brahm-Ha-Bra-Shith-Ba-Ra, which creates the earth as spirit in its dryness.

To contain them you must become the body of these. The same as that, that illuminates' life.

Khan Gu enters unannounced. His face is filled with grave concern and the desire to move things forward quickly. His nature

contains a sense of urgency but his spirit does not desire to excite the others.

Caanon

But what are the arts?

Khan Gu

There are seven arts.

All turn startled at his appearance. All stand and salute with the 3-4-5 Triangle sign. Solei addresses him.

Solei

Arama Atitich Khan.

Khan Gu

The seven arts:

- *The first is the instruction of the firmament, of the heavens and earth, and the primeval order of her people. The canopy of the Heavens and that relationship it has with the center of the Earth. We draw by it the powers of the Universe. That power is in the center of every universe from the atom to the star, to the Golden Hiranyagarbha.*

  It determines our political life as monarchy as the center of all law and principle, as well as those who are sages who are the center of all sacred institutions.

  There, in the stars, we have the spirits centered by the company of the Gods, or those lives of pure energies in superconsciousness, and the elements and powers that fly by them—even beyond that

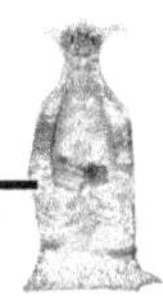

touched by light.

They effect creation, space and the superior intelligences through the hierarchy of intelligences. We are One in that spirit of Super-consciousness. We in them, and they in us.

We are bound as One in the energies of Superconsciousness and we are shaped in that spirit of time, motion and the infinite cycles that form, by the Fourfold Name, as Spirit in the Egg of Cosmic Illumination.

- The second art is that compelling the first essence of light, breath and thought. It is the subtle order of occult vibration, moving from that spirit that is above. It causes its divine precipitation into nature.

It follows, these are the transmutations of one thing, as it is changed into another in the Miracle of that One Thing. That is the revelation of the One Element appearing as the many.

It also includes the knowledge of the stars, and the meaning and virtue of their nature. These appear in their intelligent causes. They form all things in creation.

Righteousness is the cause for all that comes into creation from this. So, in our meditations we confer in arts and sciences, and realize this as our subtle cause for existence. Our lives are influenced and shaped by them.

We may examine these energies, beyond their basic elements and light vitalities, by traveling in the state of Cosmic Consciousness.

By this we can realize their intelligence and dwell within the nature of their wisdom. It is experienced as the life that is lived beyond the sensual form.

God, beyond the infinite, has no distance, and cannot occupy any place, any more than to say that it is in all places. There is no sense of space. It is singular as the live spirit that is One.

Every One has a center. The space-less has an "any place," as it has an "any number" being omnipotent, omniscient and omnipresent.

This is our experience; even beyond the stars. They exists with the starry gods hidden in their Mysteries, being themselves the beings of the centers.

They are as a twinkle in his eye in the Great Anyplace-Anytime AB-BRa-AM-oN.

Khan Gu is weary, old and near death. He moves slowly to find a place to rest. Time has taken a strong tax on him, for the lifetime of his powers given, and there is yet another duty yet.

Solei helps him to a place where he is seated and she converses quietly with him, and then she appears suddenly concerned and continues.

Solei

- *They consist of the powers of divination seeing by the light of subtle thoughts that know all of this, from the supreme consciousness, without the former instruction of their instruments, and they live by seeing into the secrets that are hidden and obscured, that conceal the spirits of imagination and reason, as in the power of subtle seeing, in all*

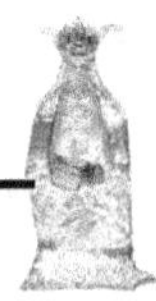

time, past, present and future.

Time exists in the future, and comes from that place as it moves into the past. What is caused from the beginning is known from the beginning.

The seed is planted then. We see by appearances only that power presented as its first unfolding as the rose or lotus form.

This is a simple science that causes the person to speak only that truth which is impressed upon it by that virtue, drawn by Time in the sacred voice that follows it, as the conscience in the light.

It is born of wisdom and the Voice of God that speaks from silence that is incessant.

It is centered in the throat of Man, as the God of Sacred Voice, Bra-Ham-Ma-aHa, and is the evocation of the breath.

It develops through intuitions, dreams, speculation, fantasy, myth, bearing with it the natural affinities. In the most profound it appears vast and powerful, through the realization of the Mystery.

- *There is the science which deals with sidereal bodies—Being the self-born wisdom.*

It is the Wisdom without flesh and blood, but rather the consciousness of light in celestial bodies, and the visions of our realities that fly, by them, as Astral spirits, and their living principles, that form the embodiment of all celestial entities.

They are the primitive super-celestial points of ideal generation, and the source of power and gravitation forming the Intelligences.

It is the revelations of their spirits, and the containment of the life, in the light, sporting all self-generation.

They are us in that state beyond the flesh. We are not the body. We are as they are in our first state. We are one with them. Our flesh is a form that is a sidereal hysteresis, shaped by these intelligible qualities.

Upon the face of every science lie the signatures to the state hidden in the art. This consists of the understanding of our ontology, through the signs of light in earth.

It is the symbolism of the reality of Light, Life and Love; expressed within the juices of nature.

These give their lives in sacrifice to us, by producing their life healing energies.

- *Amid these qualities of the spirit, there lies an uncertainty of arts, which deals with prophecy or the foretelling of future events upon consulting fire, water, air, or earth—and that, though difficult, proceeds principally from Time factors that point to them.*

It is seen by the imagination in that psychic sight and is absorbed as prophecy, in projecting changes, and the course of their directions, and they are dependent upon one's inner faculties or internal attributes—they are reflected upon the elements, and the changes that exist in time.

These lie concealed behind dark flesh and senses, and are often whispered by the conscience and inspired by the intuition.

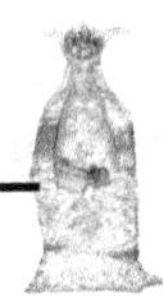

- *The final art is that of the physical nature and manual expertise. This deals in writing, or instrumentation, geometry and emanation, and the relationship of the internal and external sphere of light, and to measuring and weighing and secondary sights.*

  It is the magic found by the duplication or replication of nature's instruments in finite creations, or in the work-bearing implements, which by their nature cause the transformation of light and darkness, into forms that appear as in their representations.

  These exist in order to collect information as a secondary form of experience, so that we may use these properties of nature in other subtle ways.

  These are not true experiences or Mysteries, nor images from the truth, but are a form of secondary sight that can be put to good use by our sciences.

  They may be false appearances, but their general uses are acknowledged as useful to assist us, due to our physical limitations, and our having to subsist, existing dependent upon the five finite senses.

  They are extension of these senses. They are our excuse for ignorance. We cannot depend on them for knowing anything. They are instrumentations that help and support our lives for living in the senses.

This ends the lesson. Solei gathers up notes, and with a nod from the Khan, she and the council members leave the Temple quietly.

Khan Gu

The children of the Kingdom of the Motherland are the totality of the sounds of nature. Each thing under heaven is limited unto the sound with which it was

created.

Not so with each of us. As Lords of the first power of the light we stand upright. Each person possesses within themselves the power of nature in the mineral, creature, plant and animals as the instrument is given, accompanied by The Word of God and the Powers of Meaning.

Invisibly by the numbers, these letters, and their motions, transition through all imagery experienced through consciousness, in the spirit of Mind in light and darkness.

The animals and creatures, plants as well, experience it, but by their limits they are not engaged in the vast knowledge of the stars, nor the Word of God. Theirs is the spirit of the limited intelligence.

Our obligation is to divine the meaning of Truth and Righteousness, by The Word of God that lives within us, within the light in us, in the power of knowing. That knowing is given dominion over the creatures to know the Lord of Earth, as well, it is that intelligence and wisdom from the Universe and beyond.

Ours is to cultivate humility and cleanse the crucible of our lives. To perform duties and live in faith, and restrain the senses by turning our lives toward the right cause for the ideals supporting our sensibilities, and fill our lives with love that supplies our union with divinity, and serve others supported by our sacrifices in the laws of chivalry, while sharing our experience.

Our birth in the Word is sacred. We think by this and our words have meaning. Without this there is no wisdom, reason or intelligence.

The sounds of the Word are in two groups. Those

spoken and those unspoken. The unspoken relate to God and are the Male. The spoken to the Mother the female power or emanation in the light in the Soul of Man.

These are the consonant and vowel structures and they break into the powers in the breath or vital winds, and their methods are shaped by their rhythm. These may be written into song for mantric liberation.

In creation, we find God as the familial entity. This is our true relation between Man and the gods. The male provides the seminal seed. It is the female that provides the sustenance, in the womb and egg, and the power to give birth to the life in the sperm.

The sperm is the first design or archetype, that carries the future ideal of the unfolding creature. The sperm holds the key to the plan. Without the sperm, the egg is lifeless.

The sperm sports the original from the divine male ideation in the form of God. It is incarnated into the male and female forms of life.

In truth, the only male is God. Creation is a female form, which is why it is labeled as the "Ba" for both female and soul attributes. It is the second and it is silent. It is the first form from the lips, that supports the Word of God.

The Mother is the Monarch of the Family life. She carries, gives birth and is the support for those who descend from their mating. She is the first to feed and is the first to sacrifice her blood in the birth and in the milk.

All are part of each divine family. The Divine Male is the source of sperm or seed. This is the first conceived

in the alchemy as the male aspect of God's divinity.

The Mother in the creation is the womb and the nurture, or the nurse for these. She is that spirit moved by the orbit of the moon, and the atmosphere of breath in air and the watery element. These are the life principles that capture the vitality and store it.

The elements form beyond the stars and even beyond Hiranyagarbha, the Golden Egg of Life, and are broken into four groups or even five; as representatives of earth, air, fire and water as well the spirit, depending upon the strength, the intention of usage, and particularly with relation to their sounds in nature.

They are the first forms of ideation and numbers, that unfold as that which is more-subtle than nature, though they are the cause of it. They are the faculties of God. They expose the divine in ornamentations.

By these all of nature has corresponding places in universal classifications. They are the spirits of the "Living Things" as creatures that exist, within the Mind of God.

The voiced sounds are representative of the powers of transformation, within the realm of thoughts; extended into their powers of accomplishment, as the self-caused entity has inspired them. This to our astonishment, as they are also revealed in the forces of nature by every aspect.

In the divine assumption of their universal nature, the letters assume the divinity and its elemental, zodiacal and planetary attributes. These, as the spoken word transforms the Great Mother's miracles as virtue.

In this assumption, Man is God. The same. This is the secret magic art that is the power of the Light of Life.

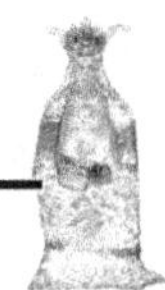

The Khan breaks his thought and walks toward Caanon and Sheea.

Khan Gu (Cont'd)

This is enough, you are well prepared . . . What can be done can also be undone! This is why we must test.

Caanon

There is so much to learn. All is lost, including this wisdom with the closing in of old age, and there is so little time given to our lives.

You are the living record for our wilhom, and our remembrances that are all soon to be forgotten. If you leave, will you come again?

Khan Gu

So little time?

Sheea

Yes.

Khan Gu

Ah Hah! There is an eternity.

Pausing, he walks off without listening as these others speak with no one listening. Standing, he begins gazing as if looking through a window or vision into the atmosphere, seeing beyond the stars to determine what secrets lie behind their light.

Khan Gu

Sacred to mortality, Knower of the Known, I hear your sweet Mother's Mystery calling by that voiced clarion.

Sung, greeting atmosphere from the heavens and beyond.

Garner up thy Mysteries here tonight. Delight by this our moral destiny to present the Table of Truth in their colors lighted by that miracle, patterned in the grip of Time.

Sing loud clarion! Lighting that voice by those embers, seeking, ever-creating, everlasting, while producing, this placement of this live Tablet of the Stars.

There appears to be an opening in space that begins very small and it grows in size appearing vast, as if space within the atmosphere is hollowed out as endless space, and behind that the Atma-sphere of endless emptiness appears.

It is likened to a hollow cave seen into as blackness, and within that hollow light can neither creature nor element enter or escape, from the blackness, since it is that depth beyond the light that swallows it.

Khan Gu stares for a long time, as the depth of space opens into the blackness of a profundity, revealing the powers hidden by the will in unreflected light.

There appears to form first a vast platform. A great tablet is spread across the universe, as if the surface of the sea were created as a Tablet Entity.

It moves in undulations, like the sea of waving forces that roll past squares that are shaped rhythmically, and sound is passing through it, as it is organized by letters. These transitions encounter the square edges as if pounding on four shores.

There its surface, flowing through vibrations, and it is cut along a single Fourier plane and transform, complicating the equation by cutting through the sound as voiced illumination.

These patterns were placed in outlines in the perfect pattern of directions, and they were governed by the signed greetings of the

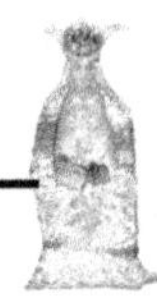

elemental signs, in the division of light. These come from the light of intelligence and wisdom, from the cosmic stars, as a superposition of expanding spherical waves radiating outward, and expanding forward with a curved phasefront. These define the amplitudes of different possibilities for space in different states This was synthesized as sung from an infinite number, as a modal form of nature, pushed by the plane wave phasefronts in their orientation, in different directions, expanding into space as a ball wave that defined the zodiac. Time and Space equating their planets and their stars.

Within the center of this ocean, there arose the lady like a mountain out of water. She, *Mer-E-Yam*, was the sweet Mother of All Mysteries, the one who forms the cosmic stars, giving them their sacred shapes and fiery attributes.

She, rose climbing as if grown suddenly out of the clear waters. She was as a miracle rising from the center of the spatial frequency from the tablet's art.

She was the most beautiful. There she appeared as a spectrum seated glowing, and by the sea's plane wave mode, her dressing colliding and rolling ceaseless, she was markedly revealed in her blue dressing's flow.

She began her speech as voiced chanting to the stars. Some sounds were vast droning, as vibrated crisscrossing waves the size of galaxies, others tiny shaped vibrations, with the spirit of quick pacing, as that of the honey bee within the hive.

Hearing as one would hear if hearing these, their honeyed voices streaming, vastly buzzing, voices smearing, as is heard by buzzing speech, when heard in tiny time.

As she chanted the waves rolled as if across the ages, and where they crossed along the plane of her superficial places, the letters appeared in the pattern of the squares, lettered by their qualities.

Light scribed space-time as a waveform propagating itself through

free space in a vacuum. Then rushing through starry material mediums, they formed classic complex quantum wave functions. These were involved in speaking quantum states, fascinating by their degree of freedom in position-space. Of all voices they were spoken in momentum, which formed from zero spin to infinite, and their points formed complex values, forming columns that were growing, by the supreme superimposition of the loaded lotus states. These in complex output beams of place and time, were seen as growing into space, becoming vast and beyond human reason, and analysis of vectors in vector fields, or interpretations of vector sums, in their infinite sinusoids.

Determined by their qualities they appeared in the natural order of their creation. And, there beside her seating, there appeared a giant obelisk, rising from her as out of a graveyard, just to the right side of her. It was marked by the signs of writings from many ages.

These produced the nexus of man's relation with the stars, as if spoken for the ages, before or after their first meetings between God and Man divine.

She began to speak their meanings and these meanings were her blessings, and these, by sacred numbers, contained complex ideas that were unfolded in her message from the stars and the Word of God.

These appeared, formed by many ancient and strange languages, and each language was written into layers that were translated at least three or four times. This by well drafted labor, but these appeared instantly. They were sacred both to past and future times.

These words that were written were there to explain the tablet, as laid down revealing many lessons of the stars. It formed the summation of all that should be known, or could be known, in the instant they were written.

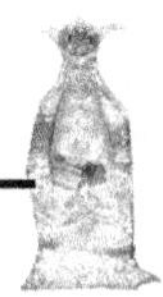

There suddenly from that sacred place, Time stops, and she begins to greet them from out of the constant chanting state, in a language understood by them to test their worthy entry, into her timeless place. She was a mystery of sacred memory as she was there seated in her role, in the Cosmic Consciousness.

Khan Gu speaks for Caanan and Sheea. But his voice, at the first, is singing melodic mantra as poetic lines. This to address her place of beauty. She could only be spoken of, because she was too much to know. She was Ana-Anta Hoa-Ana Hacoma, the Goddess spirit of an animus unknown.

Khan Gu

Hoa Ana Goddess of love and song
I hear that echo of love, Fair Faced,
And by this you have love enthroned.
Enthralled, you are glorious, and I savor this.
Our delight recalling your face, your voice, your song.
To fall, we before you, as the Goddess of Songs, hearing
you here now as brighter than the nightingale.
Forestall us to come. These songs of Love that are
recalling us. To the Songs of Love, that are as God
calling to us.

Lord, was there ever a Mother seen like this, whose eyes
outshone the stars, or by whose touch we would be
blessed, to a tenderness that would last for lifetimes, if
only by her blessing.

Seated before her veil, smeared by hidden tears of love.
Her bliss enjoyed. Whose love stood fast across the ages,
steadfast, as solid emptiness, before walls of torment and
fortune over Aeons descended in the fall.

Blessed be her name as I pray it! Ana-Anta Hoa-Ana
Hacoma!

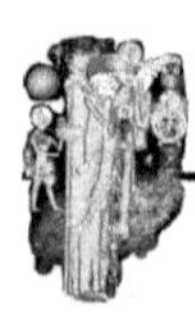

Her name is, by virtue, represented, by every letter blessed. Blessed She. For She is truly in, and beyond all blessing. The Aeons are turned by her numbers. By Ages she calls out Time-Space to adore her. Damned are these to come again, but blessed to live in her record.

Born, we are, into Intelligence by her delight, at the experience of Her Eternity, we are garnered with insight. She is discrimination, reason, judgement and clarity of vision.

For Eternal Mother dear She is, sweet Sephirah. Born within, no as the macrocosm, to Be forever unfolding proper order sainted mother, Saint Bea-Nah.

Her mighty ocean, tremendous wakes of love, and most powerful sea of invisible persona, divine personality. She is the omniscient and Immortal Sea, beyond all Immortal Senses seen, single sensed, as the "hearing-vision."

Our breath is taken. I cannot breathe. There she stands before us here; the Lady of our Birth as she was before the sun appeared. She, who bends our soul in her company, to witness her, as witnessed before the earth.

She reflects our love, as we appear unto her, declared as best born, to come born in love with her again. Breeding by her lunar lights our lunar faults and lesions. Our wounds laying here as treasons, open wounded failures in our lessons.

She, upon the wake, that rolls by another hour, is like the spring, whereon one's tomorrow's flower, Lotus like, or beside our reason as the ever-unfolding rose.

To love her is to set one's heart into flaming fire, with burning love in life's burning sun of ultimate desire, and there she entertains the experience, as if it were of lovers unremembered who have returned again. Prodigal, in

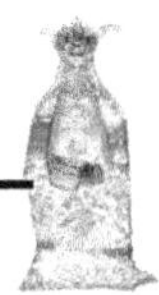

long forgotten temperaments. She remembering, forgets.

To sprout; again, as now, feeling suddenly alive! As the seed that sprouts to first meet the sun, and she by us, being be born one again before the source of love, Amon-amen Ehyah Raya-Nara-Naya, as her emanation.

The sweeter seen, from her world grown flower, we are standing by. To be sliced by her shaft, used to cut her flower, and draw the rue apart to find the center. From the worst and best, we are taken out of every hour, and sifted for what is worth. She cuts the Jewel, of the Truth Aegis.

In the breadth of human aftermath, we'd wake after such Jeweled Age, of life. To sigh these verses from our mouths, too weak in their weary cries, of each age passed, and here sought, to flower for a day, by reason born of judgement. And we called here to defend it.

Her voice amidst this ink, from this unworthy pen, and I as heir to its writing. I may script the voice she sings, or recall lived life, lived again in all those voices, so learned to hear, yet we cannot contain the value of their listening. Since we hear all of them.

The sound of Time. That, here marches timed paces. As here she is portrayed vibrant, vibrating first before us, the veiled as witness witnessed, and her time beating, the gong drumming thunder into us.

To those sounds heard, they transform unity, into existent triplicities, with changes breaking time.

All born in the song of time ringing, "Te-King," within the winds as the winds in their wind-ing chime. Breathy speeches of vitality, they begin their wandering way.

We stand by their hours stretched into eternity. Our

world to be torn asunder.

I pray, "Ana-Anta Hoa-Ana Hacoma, wise, I by my down-casting eyes, am charmed by your call. Hereby I plead for these two, the Children of Truth."

She revealed to us her backsided glance. All, inspired by the sounds of her throated gargle spilled lines upon the field and by her gander, we became the wise enticed to wander.

To hear her voice. To clear that fading wind from the mind, that is unreflected by her voice of daylight.

What shadows were hidden away are now revealed by the celebration of her winds. Of the old worlds, those now recalled from natures vision once again. And the Master of the Image, reared as birthed from a whirlwind out from the center core. Coming out, from the depths, of the self-sacrificed center once more.

And, to all the lands on earth that were formed, that we stand or have stood upon, from the dust of listless earth we wandered on, we suddenly remembered. We desired to quench, what was hot tempered, and we set about to conceal the worst.

The chided childhood of Man has yet crackled old aged, into the wrinkled old and wise, and nature has prevailed as ice forms upon the vain guise of long lost forgotten lives.

What a witness. Thy son's and daughter's life of generations of wickedness, are cracked when the once sheltered forms, now opened. We are pressed now, about to run away.

Our fair virtue fain's us, willingly about to retreat, from our unworthy recall. Of life revealed, before our venture,

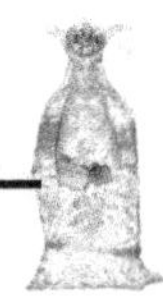

near fallen as you may be one appalled.

We fear by our vicissitudes, what ill fortunes we may have done, to take us to a creature, crawling in our embarrassments.

Rejected in Nature, now, this would see us the saddest creatures ever seen of all. Blinded by ill progress, before the scores of the wisest of our breed.

Saints and sages as seen, who would know this world, may be pleased to see we are the victim of wicked stench, for the smelling drawn from the world below. We may be among those unshowered though unrepentant.

Glistening in our fires. Our lighted bodies, fresh born, have come out from the world wielding the sun of our earth flowered.

So that the Greatest of All, the Lord of Earth Adon, is now suckled in vain vanity arguing before us, as our legal representative, come here to witness ourselves, and yet blinded to our injustices.

Claiming for us saying before retreating:

"As the world wailed unfoldment on the sheltered that ran, while the incumbent Time, its unfolding hour began.

"A diamond in time will again be found to find its fame, as a period of grandeur; where mind will reign, and from out of the earth amidst startled suns, the cloud bearing warriors here, were stalking the proud wearing psyches of life who were not alone. Many followed.

"United together, the world will reveal the Self-ingrown. To yield the fresh and promised retreat of those retreating, when finally known. To these we plead, gather them together again another time, these vagrants, to sit again at holy feet repentant."

Now before our being called to gather members here before us again, I pleaded for our canons that were prepared for defending Caanan and Shea saying,

For from out the thousand eyes, God has watched, to crucify our lives, in deaths that are real, forthcoming, but not perceived, by our prophecies tonight.

Selfish wants. The need to progress, through Self in deeds. These are needs to compound the heart in its love conceived, in that core born with the call to chivalry.

Toward Self, and those selves tuned through deeds that we may understand the need and necessity of life and the lives we lead. This Self stands here now, laid before you as a book that is opened wide. Nowhere to hide. I have given myself to your judging labors for my life.

Immortal impressions fulfill this hour of the soul. To flaunt by it, our breath last breathed from whims, to become the grace, to bless our spirits bold. Only you have the power.

To expand, we are one mankind, working through our stinging wounds. To be expanded by courage with the age of chivalry, self-sacrificed, in thoughts, words and deeds.

Placed now, we have come to face the outer god by the goddess, and you reveal its destiny. It is the matter taken of the heart.

When you, when I, in union came to life, we witnessed to proceed unjustly prepared. We will not do this to them. This, as sensed is the provenance of my soul, by its Master-Mind. This is what is believed.

A million windowed hearts as eyes, we will install these here now, hereby in the hopes of receipted blessings. As

witnesses who witnessed us first. In the One House, in the Blessed Kingdom, where we are called to rise and fall, in old lover's eyes.

Though we peer without their solar windows now, through the suns staring in the starry nights, we are sworn as seen without the kingdom, we stood before the gods, under clear skies, and all with our oaths sworn that were taken. We were not hid, or hiding out before them like those who sneak about the night. They have witnessed us revealing our dearest content in our character.

But we rise only to peek again, through their prophetic eyes, to see these coming days that are soon to fall.

We beg the forward moving eye of coming wisdom, by that assistance of intelligence, to stay our lives in hopes, witnessing in this to survive rest and peace, by your grace and by your deliverance.

It is due the world. Beyond beliefs, our pleasure is the sad grace to rest in peace, only as death alone finds us leaving in sad graveyards in the end.

Therefore, I plead before you that for these two, and for those more who will come. Their passions as well, or else to waste by these, the corrupting seeding thoughts of love may go unsprouted.

For us, to speak reflecting plainly before our hearts, confess our unsuppressing thoughts. You may see them, they will not be denied, question us. Withholding by authority only those thoughts abolished or by silence stopped. To avoid saying what cannot be said.

They may be experienced, as seen in Light, experienced in God, but for us, we have come to experience true blessings of peace, life and love.

These are lives we must live yet again. Unfortunates, but with hidden records, for silence becomes us in our private thoughts.

Settle, my inward Lady into that gentle state. For fear in us to reveal ourselves may silence us. Relax within your peace, the vows of harmless gratitude for us, with ours with you.

Unto their minds, these two, release thy pledge for peace. My heart breaks. This is my chivalry.

Faithless, yet is their virtue hungering, when the best is known only to your grace, it will be known again. As sovereign Queen before our humble names. We are naked as named here, "the pleading."

Awaken then peace dear Lady and draw your mind in this, our simple natural vein, that mines its way to freedom.

Liberty is the only means to our escape. By free will, we will come to love again. In that happy state.

Tunnel in and flow without, the greatest good will come. Here we plead to awaken that simple gratitude, to draw these two out, sustained for their simple needs.

I see here by your field of names, water flames as water stars by your grace, wrought from out of the patterns of this night, as thy mysterious hearth of stars are lit by water lights.

Scintillating flames in thy charms delight. Gather together in flight, and fly by the moon. Call out the dew in the air in the mists of night and we may draw pleasures by its wet alchemy.

Passionate Lovers, two here. Nature's twins, by the heavens are transformed to conform for our futures as if

this be their true wedding day.

Gather up the dusty wetness in thy white-water form. They are together tied as twins to live, as motion in thy wonder, male and female together.

Together, they will in wonder wander in their purposes. These two lovers trapped, enraptured, imagine the world, by the little they have to go by, be kind to them.

What matters to them, is not gird beside them with the blade and hilt, but the love that's about to be the way forward from here. We wish only a safe journey. Be their comfort.

As the mother that cuddles the babe, you by her, may she in you recall and understand our labors, to give birth by your love, remembering her love and her loves made, for you, Mother of mother's, had a mother.

As the form first, there is the gift of love wrapped by the child that comes with age, for the thing that love has made, remember these.

As the cycles turnabout with every day, she the mother peers out of that window to the world, that is cold about the house, and even when there is snow upon the ground, she is love, hot without, and she remembers what a lovely thing has passed the night, by that, once touched love esteemed, to bring this "all-loving-thing" about.

The Great Mother is first silent long. Khan Gu has finished pleading for himself and then for Caanan and Shea for their blessings and for their journey to La Mayach. After some time spent in meditation she speaks to those assembled.

Mer-E-Yam

In my judgement all travelers must be tested. Therefore,

questioned. So . . . Who is worthy to Speak? Before me, you are my spouse, you may prepare these for the future generations then.

But answer husband, before we are crossed. Who is worthy to know? Who is unworthy.

First, speak. I Am Eternity in thy wonder, as Wonder's mate.

They will come begging of them. They may judge or be their guides. But how will they know them? Who are the first-born coming out of the Darkness of Earth where they go descending into La Mayach?

Khan Gu

By your grace, here beside us in the world, they who are those who are the selfish, conceited, proud and arrogant; who are those called first-born, coming out of Darkness.

They are those who are living false lives and defaming peace, truth and honesty, who with their disregard for wisdom, are living lives of jealousy and envy.

Pride declares itself false, by these false-faced, though unwanted and envious, and it transforms divine powers into bad tendencies, and by these vanities without life lived in that peace of generosity, they display shows of greed and injustice, anger, rage and hostility, before both friends and enemies alike, and so they are all deemed unworthy. They may not come into La Mayach.

Most are as children led by the idle minds of false generations.

Their lives are demons lived without any form of equanimity, and their hearts have disregard for the true compassions, of the compassionate; pretending to do

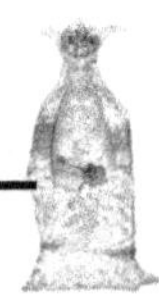

good, by their false remembering.

These false-faced values have led them to bad tendencies. They show the demon as the man driven by the desires, harboring guilt that is shadowing the mind, and leading it straightforward into great wickedness.

They attack where love should prevail as those who are given to follow laws and principles by their academics, books and ignorance.

Mer-E-Yam

Who are those that are cursed?

Khan Gu

They, unwelcomed, are those cursed who willfully step forward to break the divine commands, rules, laws and principle in their ignorance of values.

Truth and justice, is shamelessly unlived in them without regret. These shamelessly live lives that are regrettable, as in those shamed to indifference.

They are cursed who know nothing, and do not seek to learn, and then they keep bad company, and live among those shameless selves, as those who live the life of dark indignity. Stupid!

There are those who, by knowing nothing, also stand by as those who pretend to know everything. They are regrettable and unwanted.

And then, equally, those who know much, but share nothing in that sea; set dreaming and sitting conceited in that selfishness.

These all, equally have failed to encourage wisdom in any other. They may not enter into La Mayach.

Mer-E-Yam

What lives are those written down in my Book of Books as demonic.

Khan Gu

Those who are deceivers. They are those who cheat, lie and steal and believe these are truly sought as a means for truth and justice. Those who belie what is harbored as truly good, where that is truly forgotten in the being. They are as the dead.

Being the immoral they fulfill lives as traitors, conspirators and defamers in society. Sneaking, as dead things that are seen as crawling demons.

Disloyalty to the good is an evil disfigurement in nature. Loyalty is divine. But, loyalty without reason is an occupation employing foolishness.

Wisdom, that is divine, is not wasted on deceivers. It flies from their very heart as darkness in the shadows stalking for deception.

There clamps the tale of darkness around the neck as the noose around the wretches of wretchedness.

The heart, mind and tongues of those who would be saints and sages are first tested for these tendencies before setting foot before thy graces.

Mer-E-Yam

What is greater in the world than wealth and acquisition?

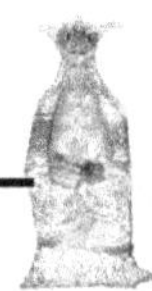

Khan Gu

The mind that moves on, progressed in links day by day, to change good deeds and thought into actions moving into the ever-onward light.

Who's to know much less remember, an actual right or wrong word? When motives change with daily deeds to bless one's inner sanctum.

This mind procession, proceeds by ups and downs to revolve into one day, then turning to revolve into our Masters by ending nights, when seen in rising suns with the daylight.

Forgive them who seek false wealth.

The poets, prophets and the artists sense the sphere of creation lived ever here and hereafter. It is a march through time, and by these the drama of ageless scenes of inner sense, are played as pleadings for their innocence, to call out the inner master, from that unwashed inner life, that comes one day pleading for forgiveness.

To set what is right, into life as the pleasantry of eternal bounty, or wealth that is timeless and forever.

They unworthy, away, only for a while, the one life recasts its eye to light someday, sending it through time without false labor. Its new sights are those longed in loneliness, where the selfless self, has dulled dark animus, by its good works, labor and thy savor serving others.

By these, the Good Lords of Life may delight and smile from that emptiness of poverty with pockets emptied.

This new sight of someday, that always promises, has crept in upon a simple soul once lost in the diseased content of greediness.

As a tear that is shed from his heart where else death would soon decay it, he suddenly poured out pure waters from its source, once the well dug has struck it. There it came out, as the waters drawn, and in wetness it fell new washed upon the digger, to set and settle in the wetness in by the puddles of the spreading rain from the cleansing of the blessed.

Virtues sweetest breath relaxed the bliss by it and gave the wish that was given for forgiveness. Then it blew its light into the earth breeding a new mankind by it.

This is that mankind to come yet, by the Word that is thine when it comes to become One, as beckoned by the light, from the candle of this that flowed in wetness from thy love.

It flows someday in that peace tranquility, where earth is made as the heaven above it is satisfied in peace.

Sacrificial faithfulness works with that love that is mined, and one day it is brought from the depths, out of those caverns, that Love that is, beyond both space and time, but now it is confined.

So much is yet that wealth of life that it is yet unpondered though carried with it, that it is for me to still plead by this natural harmony, that is yet to come with time.

Of Broken Lights scattered and set apart, they are set by the wayside, as light before the prison of the prism, where spread light is broken I believe.

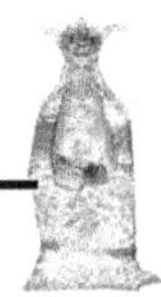

Years would cut down this ego-youth that will be lost if so short a time is given, to gain its regathering.

Their tidings of lasting peace, may not be reached if that wealth is unreceived and unguided and is lost by the way that is within them—before reaching patient heights to help that wisdom, by intelligence, to decide.

Far still too, we may go, by my Endless sight which seeks to be a sign of future virtues, reaching still by this course divine, that is ever on the way to somewhere. To talk again of future worlds and friends. There begs no words to sigh in ignorance, for there is no excuse for it.

Therefore, I forgive them, and by this I plead, temper thy judgement and mine in this. They feel, and thought emotions are there at once combined of this God of spaceless-timelessness.

When reached, it will be a place for your enjoyment as the wealth of it. So, listen hear to our answer then:

Good health and divine justice, harmony in the home and the ideal of liberty that inspires self-determination and discretion, so that it that is thought out and well-reasoned in all our thoughts, words and deeds, that gives, by every measure their peace and harmony. This is the greater in the world than wealth and acquisition.

Mer-E-Yam

In self-governance, freedom and liberty what is the foundation for laws and customs that determines the true will that defines our order that is free?

Khan Gu

Rhythm, life! Brief causes there, define justice and

add effects to crush justice, in the mind by changes.

Hope! Youth! And to live leaving sorrows far behind as it ages. New dawns follow the nights that have passed, with honors of the sun, that gives report to all, that liberty is there when the new morning has begun.

Golden rays fall to earth and winds part the newborn leaves by the winds of vitality, and each by each we are reflected on the waters like the sparkle of the stars. They rule our lives of make-believe and give to us our names.

The songbirds chime in to aspire to new life by the dawn, while the dew lifts towards the source by that heat that draws it up and turns it into atmospheres that we breathe. These are thoughts as an unformed form of animation. There it sits, between the earth and Atma-sphere. Egregore.

Between these creatures of the elements, dew, bird or star, all are in search of their ethereal sidereal rights, proceeding along their universal course which destiny decides.

All keep the beat of time and mark their struggles in the harmony with the swaying, as would the branches on the Tree of Life.

Each bend to the whisper seeking forces from the core central that vibrates the restless energies like the shaking of the leaves.

We peer now out over all this, and across our Motherland to ponder this freedom, as an outcome of justice by law, while assuming evil, when we have left that day to make another home.

By the tremors, we feel an angel stretched across the

sky to clench both hill and sea, and pray the Lord, make "A Covenant," of love between us, we three.

That angel appears first as an angel of beauty arrayed in the hopes for new life and liberty. But we challenge its light saying, "A rainbow Lord" and pray don't harm another.

Bad days ahead, a dove may come and land upon our arm, before raising these wings of law and fly away and pass beyond the senses.

We may be seated then on the mountaintop, living only by our nakedness, tapped by the rape of change, and taxed to find new hope and the place of happiness, and our ships at sea left behind will rot with time.

We will leave these for tomorrow as a reminder for remembrances that no longer matter, for those who seek and try to find. For life will live and survive on sad regrets to rebuild what is justice found by its sorrow.

It should matter little if life should miss, the promise and hopes derived by Justice and lawful order.

Somedays come. That Justice and lawful order comes with dreams of being there inspired the by the fruits of liberty and freedom.

But there is space and time for dreams to cope. Life exists beyond the mind, and its birds are carried through it by degree, to pass by the place of one's imagined charms as those birds that nestle, nesting in the branching dreams upon the Tree.

You may have felt the beauty that the trip through life possessed, or not. I may not give a damn for those who forget. What more have we to ask or expect of them?

But time waits.

When should one have expected more from the justice. They who by turns never expect less. But we expect Justice to greet us by examining all these feelings shared. For these feelings have not destroyed the laughter, the joy, the peace or that airless sense of what is goodness ever after, beyond the atmosphere.

So we pray the dove to shed a quill for our pen, to write and mystify the land, in our reminiscences. Penned to rhythmic meters possibly, to record the lives honestly forgotten across the ages that have passed in time, and that, to help us understand that we have soared beyond that breath of love, that sweetens up the lives—or that we have bathed in waters of those faithful words that are heard, from the fountain called "divine."

That sword we bear on our tongues, is made sharp from years of being sheathed with mortal bonds of lawful forms that are over-spoken on our behalf. Its blade just cuts through our arrogance, slowly defeating inner enemies that are the truly challenging horde. That battlement stands against the evil hold they have on us, that would be death to spirit's soulful memories.

Therefore, the self-governance, freedom and liberty that is the foundation for laws and customs determines the true will to define our order that is free, Lawful order, that is determined by our reason.

The divine justice and peace that is on the order of our compassion is without end, and by the will of Time it is the means for our examination, and the gifts of peace and retribution, are there listed for achieving divine outcomes.

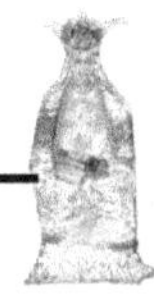

Mer-E-Yam

How is man found worthy to be loved within society when sad winters have turned away the summer, fall and spring on the solstice mid-winter evening when all have seen decay, death and dormancy? And if that Word in you is true, sing this first, as song to me and by virtue make it true.

Khan Gu

By your pleasure! Sweet. These shadows do in their backgrounds lie, false shadows fraught with Winter's resume. Of snow, adrift on the plains to fly, or rains falling down on winter's day.

Gently sung, our thought upon those that once bloomed delightfully. The night comes to life with songs of old memories—as Time removes from summers long, that day of light to darkness drawn.

Seen in rhyme the earth shadows quake, waking day. To think soon this night, by this season of our dark night's wake, will come out from gloom and winters bed, where from the cold we'd poke our nose and nod our head, and wave our approval.

To cheer this life budding as it buds again, and acting as a child would in daylight sing, and as old folks in May, who lie to each other, speaking to their hopes of spring.

And then, in spirit, wander where the thought should climb to heights again, as if a poet's part deserved this darkness to be born in light, and by that passage in subject's writ, to be moved by the spirit, to write that poet's night by it.

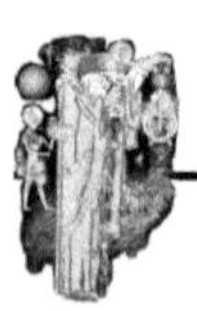

Liars everyone. Pretenders to sad subjects.

The plight of winter's. Once again, to discover life that would guide and guard us on our flight. O'er the glades of those shades and shadows, that haunt us, even by the short days revealed, and long nights yet to face. As if dark memories could, by their long shadows made, be never again turned away.

And these again, in days of spring recalled, are again called back by the shades, to the pale moonlight of winter's memory.

So, we dream, singing poets songs, with words that lie with these sing-along's, singing "Come away! Come Away!" Then tearing up.

Of a sudden there's solemn judgement, and we wake to a bright thought within, and from our dream we are delighted. We are called back again, like the hearth, bearing wood that cracks by its fires, we like the hot woods snap.

And the down drafted flue that from the hollow's shouts "hello!" to the sound of wind, coming down the cooled chimney, as the cold would bring it in, to wile the puffs of smoke by trickery. And by its puff the wood would flame, and bring us back to memory, and find us stuck within the moment.

Our thoughts of these lives, in cycles chide the smoke-filled enemy upon us, and upon the oceans of our dreams collide. And so dost our thoughts ride along, seeing perhaps the daylight in the offing, saying, "Is there truly such a day as spring?" Forgetting these are just memories.

It has with winter, brought to sadness, those dreary hearts. They come without end, but knowing soon

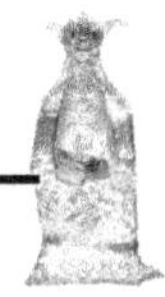

spring and summer will come again, and the stars reveal these times in seasons when they recall. We are returned to bright spirits. Not to worry.

Not I, or you should feel, so free to feel, confused to confess, or fear to start the night anew tomorrow.

As shifty praise of self be laid aside, upon the earthen hours passing yet. For by these defeats goodness is lost, as if time were cast away at the shadow's cost, tossed, and that for no reason.

That wicked thought of Midwinter's dark decree, rules judgement upon thoughts in fantasy, drawing love's lost that never were. Remembering, all of us together would be better. Distance meaning nothing.

And all the folk coming near with thoughts of blessings, in this our nature's love affair, with its destinies creeping forward, but perhaps too slowly, so boring us.

So, suddenly, as quick to pass the night we wake up to the unknown, being again where the shadows hide. We bring a light by candle or at the dawn by morning.

There again on the horizon, the hawk alighting, as it comes again with the sun, another day. That a little longer maybe, and we are there to find their fair passions turning, into life once again, what was found was hid away.

Sad smoke from ash and fire does, when proud, surrounded by the burning clay, discovered its flash of life was only temporary, and now is forgotten memory.

Then, we find the change of heart. The mind coming to its senses, has come alas, with an era of change. Time brought in the wave a wake, and these breaks,

thoughts have passed away.

On, moved on away, to fares paid, as we did to the boatman's dread, for our passing the river into happiness when leaving from the dead.

And, by our worry and work another day, we are as suddenly off to bed again. There we may dream unto the 'morrow. For dark hours come early yet, and the strength lost from the daily labors needs replenishment.

And, of course, from our firm wit, we are extended to be fatigued a bit. It's the poor mind tired again, and of course, we reminisce, it was another winter's day.

Some of us may cuddle or huddle together, bowing to our kind, with thoughts of their loves and lovers, and those of trust, with beloved ancestors that are long left behind.

Fair people all. Beloved ones. Saddened only by short days.

Short days? From the depths of the heart they are assumed here depressed, for their high regards mean nothing, while the brief loves impart lost memory.

All golden. All glitter. All Spring. All strong to stand against the winter's frost, before the warmth of spring comes, only by our remembering.

For as the myth doll doth tell a truth in old cladded wear, unstrung for that truth revealed from the heart. It is long forgotten.

So, inspiring the uninspired, there are old songs to bear this out. Sung to remember our dark and dreary old memories.

But as that candle is lit in that heart, there it remains,

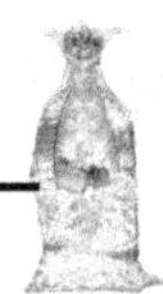

as there it reigns sovereign. It is as humbleness that is born in virtue, unstained though falsely, called out to blame the day again shortness.

By that shiftless look in the beginning we appear mortal and sin stained, wherein the heart confides in silence, the beauty of the truth, from whence we did, in our darkness hide away, from the shadows in our nakedness, as if thinking they are gone forever.

Moreover, in that light of mind we wished only to be comforted, but in the moment. Begging if found out, not to be mocked by anyone.

While thought forms appear in the shadows, they appear as only the strong spirits egregore, they are reared in mists of love that rise with the night, to call back virtues, to quest virtues missed someday, on that soul's flight, beyond those dark shadows to remember spring, forever more to summers marching strong again, with long days and renewed lighted memories.

Therefore, we may never be depressed, nor let those shadows form, to drive us through dark memories. For there it follows, you are the peace-maker standing firm by all, in that quest for liberation.

Serving others. You have a duty to fulfill.

We are finally found out. To be recovered to be worthy to be loved again within society, when those winters have turned us away from the summer, fall and spring, on that solstice mid-winter evening, when all have seen decay. For by being the peace-makers with clear reason, by our virtues, we are justified.

And by living lives fulfilled in valor and chivalry we are those helpers and guides, and those who serve the needs of families, friends and neighbors. We find, we

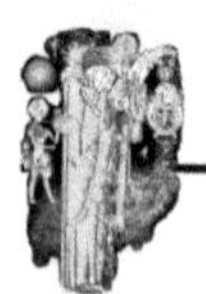

make it through the winters by being the peace-makers.

With these words, a sphinx appears from behind her dress, who is not so easily persuaded by such honeyed words as she.

It hums and growls, purring low and long by rolling double letters, and then curls up concerned for their success, in these virtues, thinking these labors are not nearly tested.

He wraps around her legs and lies behind the lady peeking as around and through the dress, as if he is secret, but demanding better answers to her questions, but in hiding displaying cowardice.

Sphinx

We follow Time in our labors day by day. Would you think to pass me by?

Pray what follows the man of virtue sage?

Fact me! Now, "Pretty Worded," for I have fated those, who come by and before me, and cause them to die, lest they answer me correctly!

Don't belie thinking me confused by pretty words as she!

Singing? Singing? And false poetic lines?

Khan Gu

Prayer and meditations followed by good thoughts and contemplation. With these a good name follows along with divine instructions that are heard by their intuitions.

These are the measured successes realized by their persevering in that honest nature in thoughts, words and deeds. These actions follow them as the wake trailing in the distance.

They are measured by the rod of wisdom and the measure of the spirits awakening. Speak, learn and test.

Sphinx

My riddle is this. What is it that is not easily found then?

Khan Gu

A proud person generous in their obligations, a young person wise in their youth and living wisdom as an occupation, and the elderly sainted, with true wisdom in old age as determined by great manners, strength and honesty. And, these done so that they are all done silently.

What are the reasons to keep silence sneaking sphinx, you hide behind your matron, Ana-Anta Hoa-Ana Hacoma Mer-E-Yam?

Mer-E-Yam

To guard against saying those things that should not be said. He, by the words has power, and they should be directed wisely.

One should avoid speaking in a way one shouldn't and in a place where one shouldn't. One's destiny is divine and the voice provides that power to achieve that destiny.

To be human is to be divine. Man can feel, think and experience by these gifts, taking one on the path to journey across the sea of time.

To ensure safe passage one should be armed with reason and discrimination, protected by one's silence one should follow the path of renunciation.

Silence will aid in the transformation, from that which is human to that which is Divine.

Malicious acts in one's thoughts, or by words spoken, effect one's peace, and lead to acts that are inappropriate.

The Will is free to do good works alone, and by this it finds true liberty.

The voice has the power to effect peace or anxiety. Why break silence with needless chatter. Through the voice one may lose one's peace of mind, or find it only again when it is silent.

Lack of peace robs one of sleep and quiet reflection, and disturbs one's quiet meditation, like the thief who removes the means for proceeding on a journey safely, once their resources are all gone.

The silent person has no enemies. The one who is silent invokes silence in others.

The name of God alone should be spoken wisely, when spoken. It is the straightway leading from, and again back to silence.

To know Truth as God be silent, until you have decided, listened and then be heard through silent meditation and contemplation, for hearing what is true.

Wait, lest the voice become cynical and the mind become lost to reason, and the tongue betray its ignorance, when it speaks by being rash, or too abundant to remove all doubt.

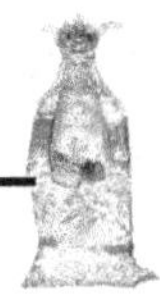

Before acting first examine and then act softly and silently. To be loud, why? When being boastful and demanding, without a true purpose, or cleared of reason for a need to be heard, is sacrilege.

Avoid sacrilege at all cost since these words have power over the elements, and their abuse is recorded harshly for their abuses. Be sworn to truth and honesty. Or, say nothing.

Who is the most silent? God is silent as the absolute from the beginning. To be silent is divine.

Awareness is silent. The personality is silent. The Soul as well is silent. It is our madness, that is the sadness, that the Lost Word and Reason are silent, and these have lost their meaning.

To approach these, one must be silent. Since silence will not be defeated.

To catch what must be caught in the wild, the first method used is to move in silence. Silence is the first art in the act of cunning, and the method used when one is hunting.

Therefore, there is need then for silence in research, since there, our silence is the most necessary for true understanding.

In silence the sunlight fills the room with light. Each dawn delights us by days of silent warning. The cock crows to wake the silence.

What good does it do him? The farmer disturbed cuts off his head to silence him. That is his reward for speaking too much? One rooster was enough, to satisfy the farmers hens.

Where the world is planted full of seeds, growth is best

suited in earth that is muffled into silence.

In nature growth is silent. The tree grows, the flower blooms. and the pearl forms in silence.

All plants keep in their places, so that nature may be silent. The canopy of stars are silent keeping their long distances, and are moved according to their times, within the Cosmic Consciousness.

Creatures may sleep or creep, but they do it in the silence.

There is a vacuum of silence in space that lies between us and the stars, for the purpose of politeness and respect for others in the Universe.

The Universe is an enormous region, but for keeping the peace we have found our place in silence.

In the wilderness of thoughts, in silence, these thoughts develop from their thought seeds quietly, since that Word that is in them is silent. When it is spoken, it is as a thought that is formed in energy of conscious vitality.

It the wood the creatures screeching are the ones that are near death, who in their tragedies are dying, for having suddenly been taken. It is the death cry. Or the ones prowling, as a predator hungered hot and hostile, or those animals rutting and driven by their seasons into sex.

These are the works of those maddened features in the lower creatures, consumed, speaking from the organs of the beast. This is not driven by Divine Intelligence.

In silence the Name of God may be known and heard profoundly, only when it is from the state of silence that it is finally spoken.

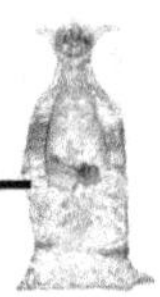

Enough, let these others speak, and be revealed in Oracle.

Khan Gu motions for Caanan and Sheea to move forward, and they approach and sit in the group. Now debates are ended.

They move forward cautiously. No one like this has ever been seen before by anyone. Only Khan Gu has brought them here by his assumption of them.

Caanan and Shea are seated in devotions, and are careful not to speak unnecessarily and have been cautioned to be silent.

Mer-E-Yam

You query in your thoughts. Ask.

Caanon

What are the reasons for speaking?

Mer-E-Yam

To ask what must be asked. To speak against the cause for ignorance in wisdom, truth and intelligence. To counsel others who would speak against these and to correct for things said that are false.

The voice is given as a sacred instrument as the Word of God, to accomplish what must be achieved as duty and true purpose.

The voice is that which churns butter from the milk. To speak divine is to become divine. To speak wisdom is to become wise. To speak with intelligence is to become intelligent.

These are the methods given for becoming what we are. The power is in the voice. To speak with untoward ignorance in debates, arguments or politics

determines that fate that is fatal to the instrument and its keeper. They are as the dead already, forgetting this life principle.

To speak is to actualize and clarify the mind, and by that then one should speak what must be known, to say what must be heard, and in a way in which it must be said, to bring comfort, counsel, and give advice as needed, and also to advance one's education.

When fulfilling purpose, as one's duty, it is necessary to ask for what is needed or to supply what is desirable, in order to send one thing or thought to another.

Appropriate speech advances one's ability to command, as one is recognized as worthy to follow another by its silent behavior.

Meaningless speech cannot be followed. To lend speech credibility, speak to others appropriately. Avoid all forms of nonsense.

The speech is the creative instrument for creating powers in creation. Divine speech gives a name and place for God that is accomplished in anything. With speech God has existence in the Name.

All names and forms become Divine when they communicate divinely, since every letter conveys the message, and the meaning, in the scope of divine language.

Dear Sheea, what is it to be prudent, wise and wealthy?

Sheea

To be rich we must save to support our needs and take

comfort only in our means. Wealth is not what is wanting, but is something that is worn, being possessed or owned. It is therefore something achieved by our labor.

But in so doing we must avoid showing the limits of our purse, or the ends of our knowledge, virtue or intelligence that is deserving of our wisdom, since all these are possessions. Even with God, we cannot barter or sacrifice what is not in our possession, even if that is an attribute. Therefore, attributes are also wealth. We should not expose our wealth, but keep it safe and protected.

We should also avoid disclosing the depth of our hearts, as those who sleep in many houses, where romance is lost to those who have no commitments and nothing is saved appropriately. They are already lost before they start.

Our wisdom and our ethics as well, should be equally protected so that these maintain a sense of value. All things of value are considered wealth.

Wealth is a legitimate endeavor. That acquired through mind, destiny, position or personal standing, as wealth, are considered to be the gifts of God, as are the favors of reputation and deserved fame, for recognition of one's acumen or attributes. These are paramount.

Righteousness must take command of one's life in the process of earning wealth, as it would one's goal for regal liberation.

Righteousness in wealth should follow the regulation as in the religion, for quieting our desires.

Wealth acquired through sources that are contrary to

divine destiny are contemptable and unworthy of our touch.

Wealth acquired through agriculture, business, mining, honest trade or entertainments, and such are appropriate. Those acquired by thefts are not.

Wealth is not something to be coveted. There is wealth in family, society and governance, love, beauty and tranquility.

We may invest in these easily. They are in our future. We may procure these also in our philosophy.

We need not bore others with either our wealth or poverty or by our over-speaking. We should act appropriately finding true wealth in its palace of happiness.

If one belly is full one should not acquire two bellies overstuffing oneself, to feed these, in order to supplement their need, or to fulfill the requisite of another belly.

Every man has one belly. Find the need for feeding in another.

If saving for the future it is appropriate to bank in that heart, where the wealth of happiness is to be saved. Without love, wealth is valueless.

Self-Confidence is of greater value, when all wealth is lost. That is when most needed.

Wealth should support education and institutions that are honest. Educational institutions should first foster truth, morality and ethics, and distribute wealth sparingly, since the parent subject is morality, and it is the cause of every instance in our lives.

One should act with a purpose to give a purpose to all

actions.   Neither wealth nor scholarship bring happiness. Nor are they exclusive to anyone.

Wealth is like the fitted gown that looks great when its fit is appropriate. We must always remember what wealth lends to us in our lives, and what wealth remains behind at death, and weigh the balance in the end, for what is truly suitable, serving the needs properly. Now and for the other life.

Mer-E-Yam

How are these regulated?

Caanan

The thought organizes acumen and power. The Word gives these powers an expression. The deed brings it under control and subjective insight and judgement.

The thought brings it into existence from nothing, as an animation of the life force that is brought into the world of actions in the cloud.

The word expresses this through the vibrations of intelligence and reason in vibrations of the breath, and thoughts become active in the deeds.

This intelligent breath having meaning, actively participates in thoughts and actions, and gives it form and expression in the outer world. It becomes a living entity.

The hieroglyphic form is an accumulated expression of the signatures of nature, tabulated and expressed and given form and meaning, in the symbols that are intricate designs and arrangements.

The hieroglyph is true and complete in form, as in a letter

or a number. They form space-time geometries. These are time-sequenced events, of word-letter interplay in a single concept. These have power in their meanings that inspire actions that determine laws and principles, emerging from the One Thing.

The intricate arrangements of the parts to the whole, unleashes a bundle of conscious ideations, in accordance with creation, and we play on these to determine the righteous interaction in the miracle.

Each of these evolve as a whole in their conception, as light coming forth as the witness to the day, and they are shared in their discoveries and methods, as the consciousness transforms itself, upon reflection in their true character, and their signatures as they appear forming in creation.

As seen, they are divided by their elemental arrangements, in the language of the gods, in over-arching properties of the power of the One, omnipresent Miracle of the One Thing, that is a singularity of power-meaning. We are the one thing, and all things relate their signatures in nature to us.

This, even at infinite or zero depth density it is defying gravitational wave beginnings, and also astral, mind and spirit densities, and the subtleties of the gods born it the field of intelligence of Bea-Nah, before approaching pure functions and faculties of divinity. Laws are determined by these.

Governing by these laws of number and letter meaning, through philosophy, we establish lawfulness in law and by these clear judgements set down to govern societies. By those who are given charge, to serve providence with clear defining wisdom, by their regulation and lawful meaning.

For every act to follow, one must possess knowledge, ability and the desire to take action through reason and good judgement.

These must come from reason overseeing the objects of perception, in order to legalize and regulate what the senses come into contact with, as these are placed in order by the mind, and are classified by the observances defining their necessity.

To learn what is of necessity one must listen and contemplate attentively and then be silent constantly, while being, by nature, vigilant; reflecting and enduring life's challenges and conclusions in debate.

In our efforts, we must regulate our thoughts with wisdom, using discretion in our discovery of what is true in moral education.

With a clear memory, we must hold on to our subjects, and turn these into eloquence when speaking, by regulating the words that are used when we speak.

To prove and reveal that wisdom also, we must hold to reason and imagination and discover improvement in the mind.

Mer-E-Yam

What is the schooling for the wise?

Sheea

The conscience, reason and intuition. These should not be neglected. These inspire the saints and sages who love everything, with their whole heart engaged, and are governed as they inspire it by their minds.

They are those who love everything beautiful, and lend

to this their strength and share their knowledge wholeheartedly, as they give their resource of ideals and understanding to the credible.

Those who follow the conscience find divinity. The conscience is individualized as the soul of mind, as the voice of the Divine, that stems from superconsciousness, and in this we find the friend, true teacher, and the guide.

It is the Eternal Witness. Knowing the true source of happiness, the conscience merges with the consciousness, that is present everywhere in that state of liberation and emancipation.

In that spiritual dimension, it is omnipresent being anywhere and everywhere, in the center that is anything, anywhere at any time.

Love is the current or energy that drives it to its destination when the heart is free of blemishes.

Reason may be faulty and has its limitations, therefore it must give way to love through compassionate observation of true principles.

Logic may not have good intentions as the premise or foundation. The intellect being academic revels in mindless discussion and debate. These should be avoided. Particularly when those premises are made up, or are rooted in deception.

One should not yield to the temptations of the art of reason, investigating truth as an opinion, or inquiring into contradictions, as a means of rendering these as their solutions as would lawyers in when lying. Each point is subjected to the lie by their parts having both good and evil roots.

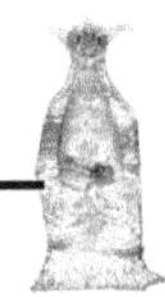

The higher intelligence transcends ordinary reason and thinking. Divine reason has its root in the superconscious intuition, with the guidance of the pure conscience, that does not disturb the consciousness, but rather enlightens it with pure reason.

Perhaps also, one should avoid speaking for others as would those who speak for puppet dolls.

Mer-E-Yam

Virtues tried. Apply knowledge and application to Wisdom—These inspire the entrance into our mystery on the Tree of Life. Also the wisdom to determine how one must apply natures laws and principles.

Behind nature lies the impeccable. The Stone of Long Life and Philosophy is hidden in its most precious metal. Its lesson is long and difficult. Only God allows its discovery. How will they endure in this metaphysics and pure alchemy Khan Gu, if sending these to La Mayach?

Khan Gu

By the wisdom of the crown hidden in the Triune Great, and by the survival of Time over the concourse over the three worlds as they triumph over senses. These worlds the gods have gifted, by the perfection of their miracle of miracles.

That power incarnates in every moment, and allows the miraculous to unfold itself in time.

Let them be questioned, they will answer. They have come prepared to partake in this, and to make preparations for the way forward.

There, time will soon be at an end. Even here now we

should be quick, for these answers to be satisfied. Time has closed in and we are nearly at an end.

Sphinx

Name the nature of the God of gods?

Caanan

BraALVHY—There is that Light Transcendent Being; transcendental by nature, imaged in our nature. That mystery of mysteries. It exists in Being as pure awareness, and is called universal, omnipotent, omniscient and omnipresent. It is the Staff of Life.

It is the light image of God in Man as a candle hidden. It lights when the dark shadow is finally overwritten, but it performs our daily tasks. It is the doer in our energies. Avoid the liars in their cages who speak of this according to their idle nonsense.

This candle may be common to all intelligibles that exist. They live according to their laws and principles, and by virtue of their pure nature's born on the Tree of Life, and by their unfoldment in elements.

Not all creatures exist carrying the power of the Word by its candle light. There man is the creature of God made manifest, by meaning hidden in his intelligence.

The creatures, plants and animals live according to their laws in this "otherness." But man is unique to them.

These are lives lived in that sense of duality, according to themselves. Universal, they appear as gods in God.

They are the "N-Te-Ra" A-Su-Ra emanations of Nature, and they are seen hidden as vitality in her

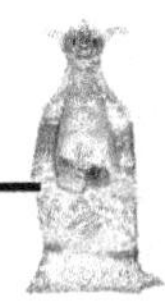

expression, forgetting their root in Ana-Anta Hoa-Ana Hacoma Mer-E-Yam. Nature is the essence perceptible to the senses, and considered by their internal measures, and their intuitive imitations.

Sphinx

How does nature compare to the Transcendent Being?

Sheea

As a mirror shining the reflection of its properties. Our astral entity surrounds us as a star. Between Nature and the Transcendent are the intelligible and sensible gods that pass between them.

They are mirrored in us. They exist as intelligences pure and divine; regulated and reflected as the light of intelligence as ordered by the orbits and movements of Time.

They are the pure intelligences, whose forces push and pull between them, moving forward and returning, giving and taking, adding properties that transition, between what is subtle and what is gross.

These shine in our organs and support the changes in our lives. We are not the bodies. We are these centers and we shine, invisible to our senses long after leaving the body as the sphere of many lights.

These relate to the powers that are sensible, relating the inner and outer senses, effecting the images of intelligence and imagination.

The Sun is the image of the Demiurge among the stars in our lives, responsible for the creation in our universe, and our starry light.

Our place is very special and unique among the stars. Ours is a living miracle and formed to provide for all our needs, as the one who created this is the one harmony, as a miracle of God. We are as the sperm hidden in the egg.

The planets are one with that God above in heaven that is beyond the stars. These creators create, in and by, all things universal, in natural conformance to laws and principles, that are unique in their nature, existing as divine creatures.

These are regulated as Time creatures, by the breath, and life winds, in the life hidden in their omnipresent root at their center. All are One.

They incarnate as number, cycles and emanations of energy, vibration and their orbits, from the Word of God.

These together form the vestment of divinity, as written by their relationship within the solar system, in transition, change, and motion. These are stabilized by the attractions to their gods.

All are held captive by their centers, in a state of bliss and love, unique, and attached, to pure or absolute awareness and identity in that one-zero-one state.

Sphinx

How can God be understood?

Caanan

To understand or speak of God is impossible. That spoken of God, "IS." It is conceived as "That" unconceivable alone. A thing we can point to.

By intelligence and reason we can only realize it, negated by that which it is not, or by its descent in the form of Avatar.

It is the Word alone that gives it life and existence, beyond the ignorance of this world, it is Meaning that is hidden beyond the forms and our terms.

It is the Word alone that describes it. It cannot be described by number, save as the vestment hanging over it, save to say it is zero, or to say that it is One.

Number otherwise implies division creating multiplications, vibration, cycles and limitations. That is the image of mortal life. The Word gives it meaning. The letters form its Time creatures.

God is not mathematical. Demiurge is mathematical as the second, or as the First Born creator god as Sai-Aton.

God has existence by the Word alone. Being is a measureless identity. As a measure, God cannot be measured. What is measured is a measure of the senses.

Being weightless it cannot be weighed. So, if you believe you have not weighed it, you have weighed it, if that weight is nothing.

It is deemed simply nonexistence before existence, since its existence is beyond everything moving that exists.

Having no existence we can identify, we know it as the "Miracle of Anything and Nothing," since there is no place that is, or isn't it.

The bodiless Naught, cannot be expressed by the embodied. Wisdom cannot be known by the deep

ignorance.

The perfect cannot be known by the imperfect, nor the soul by the mind or the mind by the body.

Therefore, it is improbable for the Eternal to keep company with the ephemeral, or those short-lived like that, but rather we are dependent on it. But it is dependent upon us for activity.

Therefore, we are gifted by its Word which is one with the nonexistent existence out of it. It is meaning evolved out of the nonexistent. Therefore, by the Word it exists within us, in the meaning as it is raised by the coiled serpent through Ma-Hi-Ma miracles.

One-Zero One is forever, and the rest of creation is in transition, between states of change that are turning divine "Meaning" in it.

Meaning is not of matter born. Churning meaning is its attempt to return creation toward its center. Meaning is therefore transitioning always into the point of infinite center. We follow it, in our daily measure beyond the senses.

The One is in Truth, the "Not One," or as "the other," and it implies that it is the Zero Identity.

You know that it exists because it exists in you in the eternal center within you that is the "I" identity in the center of the chest. It is there because it is the center that is everywhere and nowhere present, omnipresent.

Awareness that is absolute, lies beyond the Shadow of Truth, as the thing before the shadow of appearances, as the illusion of that magic of the breath covering, that is the six-fold sheath image, hidden by the miracle of form, surrounding the center that is the

seventh state of rest.

The point that is at rest ideally, is near its nucleus in the creature. It is the point of transition between God and the First Born, and the place of the beginning and return.

So far off from the stronger is the weaker, the fat from the thin, the macrocosm from the microcosm, as the lesser from the greater, and the mortal from the divine.

But as above, so below, it is the axiom that it is in Heaven as on the Earth. It is the one single period that is measureless.

As One Thing there is no reference except to say the "No-Thing," and the ignorance lies with the characterization made by all created living things, including Man, including gods, with these moral and immortal identity exceptions.

So, we end saying nothing for the question of the measure by our scale and compass, because by it we all know nothing, save the measure of those universals in love, truth, righteousness, decency, glory, honor, beauty, honesty, or those power that delight in our House of Virtue, in one form or the other.

It is the distance between the two faces, flying together in extremes, that dims the reflected vision of the beautiful.

To Know One, one must become One. That is at the final state of liberation. That is beyond us until we have reached our destination, but we may embrace this in the form of the Liberated Living, and by the power of the Stone, and in the assumption of the divine identity.

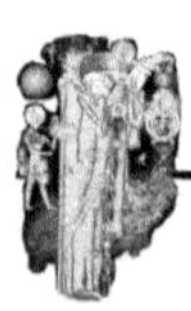

Man may be identified as God by this. On the other hand God is without limit and may come in the form of Man, or anything, as the downward seen absolute entity, who appears from age to age.

When God is in all glory beyond glory, he appears when needed, but only as a demonstration of the nature of his virtue.

There in those times mankind may have the divine exchange, for the rare opportunities may come. God may step from that unknown state into the known.

Because of the nature of human transitions, by the Word and the mind that it is conceived in, they slip into the unnatural ways, when there are defects in their reason. They will become unreasonable.

By appearances in the world of the senses, they are effected by the mind created, which may experience hallucinations, and thereby collide with joy and sorrow, confusion and indifference, and lose their way.

So, from time to time, for what is good and necessary, and for the welfare, the downward appearing Lord returns for their protection.

The mind must be cultured to see beyond the senses, to experience the virtue hidden in the vast form, in order to discover it, and therefore to be drawn by it.

Their form comes as a warning, to counsel and to guide, to lead mankind to love, and to live a godly life.

In the sea of fruit, now and then they are ripe, and these fall from the tree, as we from the Tree of Life. That is liberation.

By this the maxims may be laid down as righteous absolutes, or axioms of moral proclivity. Therefore, our

righteous appetites, by them, may be satisfied.

Though many advents have come, few listen. Regardless of this all actions must be taken on the level of our humanity, for us to transcend our experience from mortality into immortality.

This is subject to our initiation, and it is lawful as a process since we live, move and have our being blessed within it.

The five elements have been created by the will of the supreme indominable—the undefeatable. They are therefore our means of reverence and discrimination. It is the cover reflecting the divine form.

In concentrated states of pure awareness and silence of meditation, we may attune to this and invoke the true spirit of divine union, or the Divine Assumption, in a state beyond body, and beyond both the inner and outer senses, as a state of pure awareness.

This state is difficult to achieve because of the noise that is generated alone, and the powerful binding of finite energies.

But at some point Man may become as the fruit that falls from the Tree, and therefore it may separate from this in its maturity.

With the eyes only the physical body can be seen, the bodies composed of vitality, breath, mind or starry elements are beyond the senses, and these cannot be seen, except through our blindness when we examine, using other instruments to discover what is not, in order to realize that God who is existing, as the "No Thing in the Naught," is the miracle that is as endless and extreme, as it is absolute.

It is with the tongue that we can speak by the mystery of the Word. It is the Word that gives life to the spirit of the heart and mind.

Where there is love that is the first-cause beginning. Righteousness, as love, is the creator in its center, as the cause forming enlightenment of the creator demiurge.

But that which has no body, either subtle or gross, and is the pure sight of awareness that is placed behind the "field of anything," that is unmanifest and figureless, since it is being devoid of objective elements or that born of forms. These cannot be comprehended by the senses, only apprehended.

These identities are lived only in Awareness as that Mystery that is One.

That which cannot be known. That which cannot be spoken of. That is the Omnipotent, Omniscient, Omnipresent One. That is imagined in the mind and sensed only, when the senses no longer interfere, as determine by the "I" identity, before the genesis of superconscious energy, as the preexistent entity.

It's divine impulse to self-create as the Identity is externalized, and this is conceived in Time as the motion by the Word Miracle, that is the male spermatic germ of conception, forming living things in the alchemy of Sun, Moon, sea water, atmosphere, and earth.

So how do we know what we know? We know "That" only as the pure, eternal righteousness. We know it as the first cause beyond existence, because this is the experience gleaned, as we begin to approach it, even though it is beyond our existence.

We may stare from our long distance, to see that impression that is shared by those who have gone before us, who by their nearness, apprehended it.

With this the sphinx and mother vanished. The Khan Gu slumped forward where he sat and sang a song to celebrate her coming.

Khan Gu

Blessed, Blessed, Blessed Lady, sweet witness of those ancient days. Today has brought us your judgement and shared with us your blessing as comfort, in these memories.

You are the creator and witness to our lives. By your life winds we endure. Our lives, our burdens, are as deafness.

We are the sufferers now, who are, by our eyes, downcast seers. Our pain is the pain of our people, and our Motherland is about to fall to the deaths otherwise.

All about us the bounty will be gone. Our hearts are emptied. Our spirits are poured out.

Cast us out now by the music of your grace, as in the song whispered by your guidance. We may regret for longing. Missing you now dearly, our hearts are breaking. . .

But as the tear sparkles in the eye, ours like yours are blurred to glisten. Missing in not seeing.

Having seen your smile our heart dies in the final walk-away, as you are dearly missed.

Your witnessing to us and leaving as quickly, has brought this discomfort, and brought us to tears.

Foreseeing our life passing as quickly as your blessings, we forget our futures.

You are She, the Great Miracle, as the calling creature chanting mantra in those songs, sung from the beginning. Our lives are just a tiny glimmer of it.

We have felt the bliss of Universal Happiness. There are no words left to sing between us now. No support of light delighting in your garden as our lives became the symbol signs of our old forgotten memories. So there is no pleasure to be found in any of this.

In the depths, we may be inspired in our lost comfort, as would the Mother for the child who is lost, and knowing, they of that sweetness shall never return to loving arms again.

We shall accept that blessing as our small degree of comfort? Since we are wounded victims.

Come, mother and encourage us with your voice for taking our stability, and please us in these last days of conquest, by your desertion, in our ache of dividing love.

We peer silent witnesses. We are the empty shells. We are the empty voices of the long-forgotten languages.

I cannot speak these now. I may speak glib to ears with no one listening.

We are sifting through letters by those letter creatures at our loss, as when hearing the Timeless running in the ringing in our ears, hearing those great entities who are those gods of God.

But these are heard as children's voices echoed.

So Mother, hear, and as posterity also hear our pleas, for they are not vagrant whispers, but are leaves and branches from your tree.

I beg your patience. It is ours to pass on to our offspring, these remembrances are for recalling what occurred this

day.

To them we shall say, today we listened and the life winds came, as we were nearly sacrificed, in the days of the Motherland when the Great Mother came.

By whatever grace you give us now, standing by these words in their evolvement, give us safe passage, along the path of your eternity, that these two, Caanan and Sheea, may safely reach beloved shores. Bless their fleet of ships with safe winds.

As the winds today lightly touched down, and turned our hair, you came and sat wondering, for us to speak our memory, while you sat on that sea of letter changes. While we sat praying at our questioning, to let our answers be more certain.

As the life will be reflected, or defeated in our coming morning, we are blessed by fortune, to have sat and witnessed truth before tomorrow's dawning.

A smile of golden innocence, was seen across that golden face when leaving.

Your beauty sat across us on that carpet, covered by the sea of songs, written by the letters.

Creating genius, on that sea of bluing stain, with that sweet smile delighting us. While in the years that come to pass, we will be redressed on yearly memories. This shall be a special memory, honored; reminding all of us of what passed before us here.

It will be called The Winter's Dream Initiation of Death and Resurrection: The Great Initiation.

Yet too young, our ears, for us to be listened to. Too old yet to be heard when our voices speak to children.

In this period of time, where little matters, except to hear

the death song. We hear your words that sing life as hope to us, reminding, "The sea is soon to come. Then our Motherland will break away and sink."

The Mystery of Time has crept o'er the earth. Like a veil, it hides the face of fortunes.

That reveals the real. Our lives have gone dark and our vision conceals the hidden beauty.

But, though far distant, our Mother's life reveals. We hear it in her voiced song of conscience. Veiled is She by her shyness, or by that emptiness in our fingers, that cannot allow the veil to be lifted.

It holds its place despite the pain of our mortality, beyond the touch, of that nearness to her Eternity.

With our tears stained with blue bliss by her now missing sight. These tears are like yesterday's rains, that fell to nourish the earth a while.

Then by springs, they filled and flowed away, to fall within the soul, to wet the sacred roots that were spread, nourishing our Tree, and that scattered waters into their wetness, that flowed off to the seas, or disappeared inside the Earth below.

This glistening was but as the tender seedling, lighting the first delight, of these sprouting roots beside us, of our children in the light.

With Beauty's love remembered, centered in the thought. It is the glorious love, played by the sounds, flowing through the fields.

They, like waters drenching flowers, are touched, as if by golden wetness, as these charms are collecting into waters on the ground.

There is freedom. Man lives asleep. . . Within the spirits

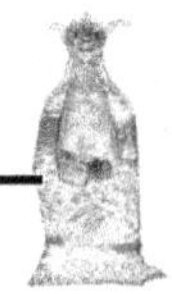

of the mind these are lived, by our angels of joy and harmony. They are the lunar silver, mined out of our lives tomorrow.

Contemplate together this digging and creeping into sorrow. We dive into the Mother's plan. I see into her tomorrow.

Now already yesterday I see by it a clear vision. And, there now again I see tomorrow.

I see this as I look out in the sea. Be quick Khan Gu, it is time to leave!

For a long period of silence they all sat quiet. Caanan and Sheea watching Khan Gu for the longest time. Finally he rose and his energies glowed in space while staring upward.

Caanon whispered first to Sheea. Then breaks the silence speaking to Khan Gu.

Caanon

Death has called to him . . . I can feel it. . .

Are you well?

Khan Gu slowly rises and walks off, but stops staring into the gardens.

Khan Gu

The splendor of this land and its people . . . my lord do you smell that . . . blossoms scent the temple . . . O how I love that smell . . .

Caanon

Would you like to sit?

Caanan extends his hands. The Khan ignores him and moves off a

Khan Gu

My goodness, you should hurry home, the pressure here overwhelms me. The sky looks dark and ominous. The moon appears in bleak blackness, dark eclipsed, as seen walking through those dark shadows in the night. In redness now . . . I fear bad weather is approaching soon.

(Caanon and Sheea look at each other somewhat frightened.)

Caanon

We are close by . . . There is only a moment . . .

Khan Gu

That smell.

> *(He draws a deep breath in.)*

My, that smells nice.

> *(Pause)*

I knew of your presence in the garden. Earlier . . . You know . . . It is as I desired . . . this meeting now that is.

You know . . . this science of ours comes from the Sun god!

> *(Breathes deep)*

MMM . . . my, that smells nice.

Caanon

Would you like to sit?

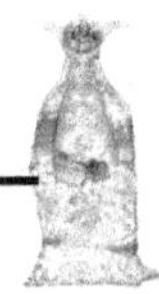

Khan Gu

(They notice a change in his train of thought . . . it is distant.)

O'no, no . . . No. You know, the supreme sacrifice of the soul, is the devotion we share, in uplifting the state of our creation.

There is truth in chivalry! More than all the arts. God is in love with chivalry when searching for the true devotee.

It is hard to find those who will do their duty. All feign ignoring by their lazy quest for idleness. They are useless.

Caanon

There are times in our quest, when my being feels like a living altar, ready for any sacrifice.

Khan Gu

(smiles)

Yes, Yes ... Yes, indeed it does that all right.

We burn our hearts, in the ultimate purpose shared, by all in sacrifice . . .

The supreme power . . .

My . . . Its getting dark there . . . such a pleasant quiet feeling. Like death walking. I should retire.

Sheea begins to cry uncontrollably, as she begins to pain—the center of her chest ignites pounding through love, fear and innocence.

It is the fear of losing once again. It has not been that long since her father died, and now this scene of another loss is tearing her apart.

Khan Gu

My hour has come . . . transition is immanent . . . I have felt the day and hour in my breast these three days . . .

It's lonely . . . I mean the thought of leaving you, my people, my work, my friends . . . I think of the work that needs to be done and there are things I must do. I am not sure how it is that I've returned here? How, by what way did I come?

If not I, who will come again? Another? Not I, I think. I may be done.

Caanon

We will miss you.

Khan Gu

(Changing his manner)

There is no end to existence . . . reality of the absolute shall always be . . . here only expressions are transitory, as in the path we share in the cycles of existence . . . I am in the bliss, or near entering into it.

I but cross the threshold, unto the spirit of the Sun, in my body glorious. There, I feel it.

I shall be as a lamp secure within that windless place, and my flame shall glow in that star, without a moment's flickering.

Being . . . Awareness . . . I will be present. And I unto myself, and to my sovereign master, shall be a living flame tending unto the desires of nature by our living memory.

(Pause)

I shall be with you always. In your thoughts. In your love. In your soul. I shall be this, threefold, as the Witness.

Caanon

Shall we retire?

Khan Gu

My children . . .

Sheea

We would rather stay, until your last breath passes . . .

Khan Gu

There is a long journey ahead that awaits the three of us. Yours to other lands, mine to another star, whose central flame shall contain my living memory. Your instruction has ended.

(He walks to a tablet set on the altar and picks it up and passes it to them.)

Behold the tablet upon which is writ the glory of the Kingdom of the Motherland! Each letter-word is a symbol which will require many more to reveal its nature.

Remember your teachings, for upon this tablet rests the masterwork of all our generations past.

Caanon

It is our solemn pledge. We have made our vows to the gods of chivalry to do our duty well.

Khan Gu

*Strive hard . . . even among the darkened times that are
ahead.*

*Oh . . . they will be dark! I guarantee it. I can see them
far into the future. They come now, as my spirit darkens
with their footsteps.*

Caanon

Upon your blessing . . .

Khan Gu

*My blessing will come. You will have long life ahead.
I will watch over you.*

The Khan moves to the center of the pillars by the door. His
countenance begins to become transformed and he all of a sudden,
appears translucent, as sounds are playing softly. The stone
appear moving by them. As heard it is like strange chanting in the
mind. He makes his farewell generous in this silent speaking.

The wind begins to blow suddenly through the temple, and you
hear the trees through the meadows, and trees are broken, as these
words spoken, come soft and low.

*Bellow soft wind that blows across our Motherlands
fate.*

*Beautiful, was your song, sung through the Crest of
our Temples gate.*

As the Khan speaks the second verse his voice grows loud. We
hear sounds of his voice echoing repeatedly in the echoes of the
atmosphere, and this voice becomes like the omniscient,
omnipresent. The sounded words are overlapping as thoughts
poured out of mind. The Khan begins to disappear coming in and

out of physical appearance.

Yellow field, sweet fragrance and flowered faces;

Dutiful unto the setting garlands, of green canopy traces.

En-Ha-Ra!
Shin-Ma!
Kalac!

There is a crash of thunder and lightning that rolls across the sky and strikes at the window. The Khan has vanished into space. Sheea goes to the Temple window to cry by the lightning strike, and to reminisce in the madness, but then she is suddenly terrified!

Sheea

[Frantic and screaming]

Caanon . . . Caanon . . . Tear away! My soul, it has lost all consciousness!

My breath! I can't breathe! My God! My God! The gardens are flooded! The sea has entered!

Caanon

Come . . .

He grabs her by the hand and turns and they move toward the pillars to exit. Vessels are waiting to fly away. Their legs are wobbling as the earth trembling as well the building is shaking.

Sheea

The tablet. Agh! Caanon! Caanon! Tear away! The tablet!

Caanon breaks free and runs for the tablet, tripping, falling, rocking as he grabs it and turns . . . Unbelievable thunder by its

sound, knocks him down as lightning roars through the temple with another lightning strike . . .

Lights are shifted and put out, and they give the feeling of the power in the earthquake with fires being created.

Caanon in the excitement falls again, and he drops the tablet. Stunned, but now standing he is up again falls down. Sheea screams frantic at the sight nearing death's approach and desperate to leave.

Sheea

Caanon!

He gets up and quickly grabs the tablet stumbling and lifts it up facing in the lightning strikes. Here he is moving as if trembling in slow motion, and his being is suspended as the moments appear like hours passing in time, as the power of Sage Time is calling him back again.

He stops. Lightning hits the temple and there is glowing light that shines upon the tablet to reveal the letters KH-A-RTzS within a circle and the Great Name: Hoa! Hoa! Ana-Anta Hoa-Ana Hacoma MeR-E-YaM.   Sheea calls out.

Sheea

Caanon ...come!

He turns, runs in slow motion to Sheea and they together in slow motion exit through the pillars as the destruction is heard. It is growing into silence.

The cloud of lights filled with the images in our scene mind is closed down, and the bursts of lightning begin to fade into the background.

There are heard from behind the clouded Atma-Sphere in atmosphere, the long flashes of earlier dialogues that are being reiterated, as if littered voices of bodies are pleading over and over again.

Time reminds us of our fears from the ancient memories. And for us we are reminded of the preparations that are coming with our return, in the coming Golden Age.

Khan Gu's voice is whistled as if blowing in the winds saying:

Khan Gu

The spaceless veil of misty wet waters, sweeps now through the crown of trees, as air becomes forgotten wind and sends it, as a vision on its way.

The mighty mountain tops, once sent the trees to touch the sun, but soon they, as well, will all be gone.

Caanan, Shea and their host have left, by that spirit where they fly, on the waves of stones of Eltron.

There is honor in this place, for it is meted justice by its sacrifice of love.

The rivers roll, one with the sea, soon to disappear, where that ancient spirit takes its flight, to greet the morning sun, to touch with angels of the sky at night; a mere reflection in its waters.

The birds chirp now, where they still breathe her life. The squirrels chatter in their wooden cages, soon to disappear. The sticks fly apart from trees, to make reply, with a clatter against the pressing wind, on wood and walls of stone.

These all mark Time.

Two feet, bare-feeted, once would skiff the earth, while I there walked, the stepping kept to its time.

While now those footprints are washed away, and

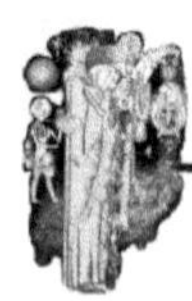

waters drip forming dewy lips made of leaves that are wetted.

They seem to sigh, "no!"

For soon they, like us, will be no longer greeted. Since all will have gone, having washed away.

I'll make a wish as I depart and send this to Mother Earth, and rush send it with my light. The sound will be caught by Nature's love, to post it quickly, and by that, before the end of night. That with ethereal peace, these winds will carry it, as once they did, from beneath those shaded trees.

All these soon to be forgotten in past memories.

It shall speak boldly to her saying on arrival, "Listen, listen, close to the voice of mine whispered, that once spoke of the gentle hope of spring.

Hear the soul at play in childish love, or hear the songbirds sing in it.

Listen! To the words once rushing to us by Ana-Anta Hoa-Ana Hacoma, Mer-E-Yam, as they were sprites of the same names, as were the waters on the run.

As willows ring now falsely rushing, as if voices speaking, they sing a lonely song, that is to bless us, in the life below the sun.

There Sun! There above, I come. You wait upon me now. I see you near the dawns horizon.

I listen to the glimmer again, with the spirit hearing in the light.

Where winds, by me, have spoken through new born leaves. They voice that once eternal life.

Where woodland gardens bloomed in May. I can hear

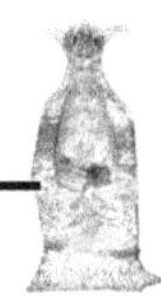

their salute to winter's change, where beats upon the winter's drum.

Time echoing and repeating, is now stepping time to tenderness. Where were those drums yesterday?

Shades of OM-Mu Ha-Mu-Ha-Ra-Anu-Aru in simple loves seeing, I would with my many faces peek before the dawn refreshed.

Those faces of ancestors who now come to greet me. I see all of them! With Earth in earth. With Light in life. We are reflected into Time once again.

Now I see the endless stream. I am not me, not one bit of me—I am Air, I am Sun, I am Waters.

Let the waters run in me. Let the Sun burn in fires of Light in me. Let the Breath be known as "What I Am."

Here! Now! I am charged as one energized, I am my Self once again!

Even now, and through the sleepy night, that, I am about to dream.

Yes, and beyond that in the new mornings light, of my reincarnations, where I may be found. But let us ask.

Now I call. "No more of me."

For, from now on my names shall be:

Aul-GeeGee-Pah, for I am the living breath.

Aul-Oh-Ho Reh-La, for I am the Law.

Aul-Hoath-EeAh-Ee Dah, for I worship the highest name of God.

Oh-Do Kee-Klay-Kwaya, for thee I stand at the opening of your creation and open the Mysteries unto the way.

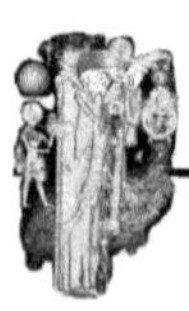

Zo-Ra Geya, Lord, dear Friend, be friendly unto me.

I am not me. For I am:

Oh Zaza-zayim Aul-Re-EL-Pa, Manin Eyah Ee Don; make me thy seer into the mind of the all-powerful One.

Geya-Eyad E AL-Kwaya-ON, Lord, Master, One and All.

To one life lived, that once passed the time lying about, now I pass beyond that mat of leaves and grasses, and settle in that matted scene of natural meadows in the mind.

Life shoots its fountain out of Earth, and with its new waters they spit into the heights.

These new waters may be in search of that universe as well, as these seas shift their masses, when cycled Masters turn to wet the Motherland tonight.

Water, air and sun become the key to break the lock; behind the Seer seen beyond the search, and seek it first, as the spirit in the knock.

It all ends here. The harmony of these three, water, air and sun, transcending even spirit, to reach the simple, at the playground centering Nature's heart, and through it, by it, our Heaven may be comprehended.

All comfort now. All eternity is embraced within the breast, we realize this and exercise our love to ensure it does exist, once we've settled in.

Far away brief speaking in those starry lights, these entities inspire, and by the death of this nation, we may yet adore, our futures, once past the storm realized, at the sign of the Rainbow Masterpiece.

Two Angels dance with the dawn. We see them now.

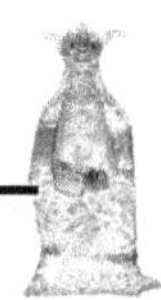

They twist turning fields of cloudy atmosphere, and these alone are together, as these two befell signs tearing mass as strategy.

They will fall to completion, by the morrows night. Dark morning's light appears saying, there are storms ahead.

Sailors take their warning, but that may be time for mourning.

One red to match the evolving rose, and the other bright, and as the lily, white. These are strange reactions in the dawning light. These are like two hands joined colliding in the wish, as greeting the lonely and the loved.

Oh spirit, walking on the sky at dawn, in this seething light, be warmed by the morning sun. These two angels breaking as the spirits before the sun, as One before earth below, and one the heaven above. These signs of challenges to be facing.

They greet us coming, as if to say "Farewell" and alone you have come to chant "goodbye's," for those who are in need. They see the signs and they respond to them.

Alone! Life, lively lived, these call to us. To call us back like those falling leaves, to belie their decay.

Where they once called these lives that were meant to plant the morning with their seeds, they now are plucked as weeds, cut down with the harvest's leaves.

Tomorrow comes by that Golden Dawn in liberation to greet the Golden Age, from dark obscurity. It will come to part these clouds, where life with needs will meet, come to express itself, and these will finally part, these elements in you, and me.

And they may come back, if they call us back again.

Fear Not! Do not think of me, but feel my words to

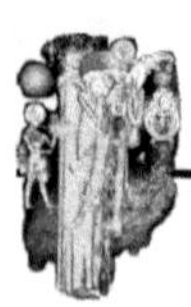

discover this life around, that walks about, within and without, to realize the higher Self, and become, along with Time forgot, as the masker, who is the caster of the doubt.

No! Be confident.

Oh Mother, sacred, who lights the fiery night with wonder, wandering in our night skies. Coming now with thy lonely self-wombs. The entombed child to soon be, in herself, slumbering, to while away the night.

Your passions swoon, midst the depth of your indifference. But so lovely to see. She who loves her womb, to announce her coming deliverance.

As the child that speaks soon, and answers back with cries. From her slumbering youth, she greets it with self-loving eyes.

She is the idiom that speaks through these, and their loving eyes, with those voices that are our fountains of fascination.

She comes, my love, with warming sensations, concerned by her commitments to be my spouse, as spoken in our initiation.

These warming sensations with her voice discovered, She comes in a breath full of Beauty filled with Splendor.

She, that touches my heart comes witnessing to me, with her forms to return, soft and tender.

And I like a flower will add life to air, to dazzle the sense of dreams for those of Time's passions, that are yet speaking, of a strong voiced love affair.

She's a gentleness felt by a stranded heart, that's been split by the shaft, and sent flying apart. As the arrow itself passes and shatters into dust.

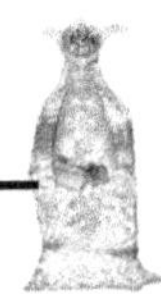

I recover again into new form, coming, from that which once was.

As One, to become ten times the love bearing field of many forms, o'er lapped, developed into finite flattery.

I am a body of many bodies.

By her mists, she forms near gathering earth, to dwell there and commences to commune in her loving childbirth.

Her passion is for giving out a name. But silently now, not so loud. As only echoes now are heard. They are bound for childbirth, and mine a new birthed frame.

Like an angel of light that's felled afar, I stand in line in light.

I am clearly bound.

I shall again light the earth. Returning to that world before me, that is stretched from my light in long distances.

Until She comes to collect me once again, from my state in some far distance.

Adding my life to the good and to the wretched alike. But unlike before, my troubling is no more for wants or dislikes, or foolish wishes.

For a passion, she has found in me, a frame new formed, of every loving kind. She is that gathered together, in the bonds of her playground, formed in the loving mind.

She the joy of a candlelight setting, is consumed by the silence. By the eye of thoughts attuned, by her mood to move forward others, searching in mankind.

Out of the sky hearing this rustle, She comes. The Terrifying . . .

The Great Mother Ana-Anta Hoa-Ana Hacoma MeR-E-YaM great, appearing across the sky—stretched across the heavens entirely. There is no day or night.

Terrifying, even so, the skies back away to let her pass. She is more-vast than space, and greater than the Mystery.

She is like a black hole formed in space, as the dark provocation. Even the sun though jealous, fears to lose its light.

She absorbs the sun and its light. She calls with mantric pleading, 'Khan Gu come back to me. For I have waited longingly for thee to come back to me again.'

Her sea waves of voice letters flowing, as a wake dramatically rolling from her dress. It moves across the sky.

She has come to collect him. Her immaculate beauty more that any sweetness, is a song. He is her melody that is sung back to him.

She is once again named, the "*Re-namer in the Endless Energies.*"

Khan Gu merges into her Atma-sphere. As a rhythm he enters and becomes a rumble through her gated, shape-shifting dress. A dress that is glowing light so bright now, that it even masks the sunlight. He enters then into her womb.

His face appearing yet, glowing in the brilliance. He is seen as a face that is clear, through her translucent body.

With body bright lighted, She expands, as she is spreading to mask the dawning light. She is extending far across that sky, and what was once the former night.

Khan Gu now appears vast. He is the hawk of dawning, when his wings of light are opened wide. That frame spans the vast horizon; merging in her light.

By her, all dawning fears appear as She stands with Sage Time, who stops by.

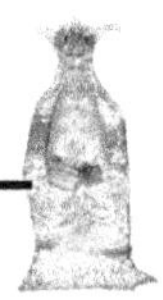

Together, they are now moving, into the forgotten spirits in the air.

Slowly disappearing. All is past. Now a memory. As Time and She slowly disappear into ancient skies.

The vast figure is blending quietly, back into sky.

She returns with Khan Gu, and even Sage Time is put away the spirit of ancient memories.

They were too busy revealing, what should not be said.

But we hear Khan Gu speak with his final words,

Khan Gu

Awake. My Love awake. I Must Enter Love Tonight. Gone, but not gone away . . . Good-Bye, great friends. Good-Bye!

www.ingramcontent.com/pod-product-compliance
Lightning Source LLC
Chambersburg PA
CBHW071246190726
48292CB00007B/2427